# MURDER MOUNTAIN

A gripping thriller full of action and suspense

# RIALL NOLAN

THE BOOK FOLKS

Published by The Book Folks

London, 2023

ISBN  978-1-80462-079-3

www.thebookfolks.com

*Something hidden. Go and find it.*
*Go and look behind the Ranges —*
*Something lost behind the Ranges.*
*Lost and waiting for you. Go!*

– Rudyard Kipling

# PROLOGUE

Early fall in the Tetons is the best time for climbing, thought Peter Blake as he watched Becky work her way slowly up the sheer rock. And doing the Cathedral Traverse with your fiancée is as good as it gets.

They were at about 12,000 feet, halfway up Grand Teton's North Ridge when the ice storm hit them unexpectedly.

Freak weather was by no means unknown in the Tetons, and they knew what to do. Peter had been almost at the end of a long pitch off Second Ledge when he decided to retreat and seek shelter, huddling with Becky on a small rock outcropping until the storm passed.

Now, an hour later, they were trying again. Becky wanted to lead this time, and Peter readily agreed. He loved watching Becky work her way up a sheer rock face, her movements a ballet in slow motion. She started back up the pitch that Peter had just come down from, using the pitons he'd left in place.

Peter had her in a sitting belay, his feet braced firmly against a rock, paying out the rope as she continued her slow progress up the wall. She was nearly a hundred feet above him now, moving cautiously over rock that was still, in some places, coated with a thin layer of ice. In a moment or two, he thought, she'll find a place to anchor herself, and then I can start up. At this rate, we should be on the summit in an hour.

He peered briefly over the ledge at a vertical drop of several thousand feet into the Teton Glacier below. Then a noise caught his attention, and he looked up to see a small cascade of rocks falling and heard the sound of Becky's boots as she scrabbled on the rock face for a hold.

Then Becky slipped.

He watched with mounting alarm as she made a desperate grab for a handhold, and then another. His heart began to pound, its sound filling his ears, as time ground to a halt. She looked him full in the face, pure terror in her eyes. And then she was off the rock and falling.

She fell twenty feet straight down. The piton which he had placed there an hour before popped out of the rock, and then she was falling again, her scream piercing the air.

I can still save her, Blake thought, as he braced to take her weight on the belay.

The rope snapped taut, violently wrenching his body as he absorbed the shock of her fall. Then just as suddenly it went loose, as Peter felt Becky's harness carabiner give way under the brutal strain. She was in free fall now, and Peter could only watch, transfixed by grief and horror, as she plunged straight down, toward the glacier far below.

At that moment, he decided he would never, ever climb again.

# CHAPTER ONE

It was just past noon on a fine blue autumn day in early April, and the Coral Sea stretched away to infinity behind his workboat as Peter Blake steered slowly through the reef and into Bootless Bay. He passed his ketch, the Laurabada, swinging gently at anchor, and continued on toward the dilapidated dock beside the rundown boathouse at the far end of the inlet.

Tall and deeply tanned, Blake's light brown hair and eyebrows were bleached nearly white from the sun. His pale blue eyes carried a fine pattern of lines at their corners, making him look older than his thirty-five years. He held a cold can of South Pacific Lager in his hand as he maneuvered his small craft through the boats moored at the end of the inlet, taking small sips from time to time and whistling softly through his teeth.

He'd spent the morning out on the reef, working the edges, probing the coral banks for shells, keeping well shy of the occasional moray eel lurking in a hollow. The tide had been just right, and he'd stayed just under thirty feet down for most of it, using his air sparingly, coming up to the surface from time to time to empty his specimen sack. When he'd collected enough of the cones, he exchanged his sack for the Nikon, taking it back down to photograph some of the coral he'd spotted earlier. The cone shells he collected were extremely poisonous, and he sold them to labs in Australia and the Philippines, where neurobiologists used the toxins in their research. The photographs he sold under an assumed name to various travel magazines, through an agency.

He cut the motor and bumped gently against the side of the dock. Throwing his heavy diving gear up onto the planks, Blake pulled himself over the side and began rinsing his equipment under the tap. He moved with an athlete's easy grace and assurance, his swimmer's body hard and muscular from months of work on the reef.

As he worked, he cast a professional eye on the puffy cumulonimbus squatting on the horizon. The morning's weather report from Port Moresby had been for fine weather and light seas. Time for one more dive this afternoon, he thought. And with luck, another several hundred dollars' worth of specimens and pictures.

But first, he decided, another beer and something to eat. He tossed his empty can into the overflowing barrel beside the tap, slung his net bag over his broad shoulder, and walked toward the office.

A drab monument to faded hopes, Edna Finnegan's tiny marina crouched back away from the harsh sun under a thin ring of jacaranda trees and a riot of bougainvillea gone to seed. The corrugated tin roof was rusted and buckled, the paint on the veranda cracked and peeling. In a corner of the weed-infested parking lot, a broken Coke machine kept silent watch beside a rusted Toyota utility, on blocks and without wheels. Nearby, a dog barked irritably in the thick heat.

Edna sat in a rusting garden chair in her usual place on the veranda, in front of the fridge. She had a bottle of beer beside her and a worn copy of *The Australian Women's Weekly* in her lap. Like the marina itself, Edna looked faded and tired, her thin grey hair framing a sunbeaten, wrinkled face that showed all the days of her life.

Back at the beginning, she'd told Blake about how she and Al Finnegan, young and full of hope, had journeyed north from Queensland, in the days when Papua New Guinea was still 'the Territory'. About how they'd brought their small savings and their dreams of the good life in paradise.

But the marina they'd bought had never done much business, apart from the dozen or so expatriates who kept their boats there and bought fuel and cold drinks on weekends. The tourist boom failed to materialize, and the big companies like Steamships and Burns Philp in Port Moresby down the road were better equipped for boat repair. So Al and Edna hung on as the Territory moved through self-government and into an uncertain independence, watching their savings dwindle and their hopes fade. Al had a mild heart attack and then another, and one day he expired quietly without a murmur in the morning heat outside the office, raising only a small cloud of dust on the parking lot to mark his passing.

He'd been in the Service, so she buried him close by, in Bomana. Because he was now permanently a part of the Territory – she still called it that, all these years later – she saw no reason to move back down south. Most of her people were dead now, anyway. She passed her days doing small chores and watching soap operas on the telly, never missing *Home and Away*, nursing a bottle or three of Victoria Bitter through the hot afternoons. Blake bought the VB for her from Steamies on Musgrave Street, by the case, every week along with his groceries.

She'd told Blake once that he reminded her of a Yank boyfriend she'd had long ago growing up in Queensland, before she'd met Al. She made Blake a special price for keeping the Laurabada there, together with the run of the workshop, such as it was, when the boat needed painting or fixing. And she never minded when he sometimes brought a woman back from town, on weekends when the Qantas aircrews stayed over.

She never understood, she often said, why a smart, strong lad like him would stay on, wasting his time in a place like this. But she was kind to him and left him alone. And she didn't ask questions.

Which was exactly the way Blake wanted it.

"G'day, love," she said, swatting a large blowfly on the railing. "Fishing all right, then?" She put her magazine down and smiled at him.

He gave her a light peck on the cheek. "Not so bad," he said. "A dozen cones and a lot of good pictures." He pulled a fat barramundi out of his bag. "And fish for supper."

Her eyes sparkled with pleasure and surprise. "You're a dear. Better put it in the fridge, away from the flies. And help yourself to a beer."

"Will do." He moved to the fridge, stuffing the barramundi into the small freezer compartment, and pulling a beer from among the dozen in the lower compartment. "Any calls come in?" He opened the bottle and took a life-giving pull on the cold beer. "I'm still hoping for one or two more trekking parties before the rains get bad."

Edna shook her head. "I'll never understand you, Peter – if you're not out on the reef with the sharks, you're out in the jungle leading a pack of bloody tourists up the side of a mountain. Can't you think of an easier way to make a living?"

He grinned. "None that I'd prefer. No calls then?"

"I didn't say that, did I? There was a call come in, in fact – early this morning. Not one of them shell dealers this time. One of your Yank friends."

Blake smiled. "I don't know any Yanks, Edna. I'm not much of a Yank myself anymore, remember?" He took another sip of beer, feeling the bubbles slide down his throat. "And what did this Yank want?"

"Well, that was it, you see. He said he was a friend of yours. From before. From Portland, he said. That in the States, is it?"

An electric shock moved through Blake's body; his stomach muscles contracted and the hairs on his neck began to rise. Portland? He felt the sweat pop out along his upper lip. Who the hell knows me from Portland?

Portland, Jesus Christ.

"You all right, love?" Edna hovered unsteadily behind him. "You've come over all pale. You want to spend less time in the sun, that's what I reckon." She pushed past him absent-mindedly and took another bottle of beer from the fridge. "That's what killed my Al in the end, you know. The bloody sun."

Blake set his beer down on the table and stood very still, trying to calm his breathing. Portland. Who knows about Portland? And what else do they know? Don't panic, he told himself. Whatever you do, don't panic.

You can be gone in ten minutes if you have to, he reminded himself; out of New Guinea in half a day. Top off the Laurabada's tanks with fuel and water, head out tonight, no lights showing. There's money and the fake passport in the boat, under the forward bunk, and a lot of ocean out there, just beyond the reef. Don't panic.

His voice, when it came, was calm, almost a whisper. "What did the Yank say, Edna?"

She sipped her beer and thought carefully.

"Like I said – that he was an old mate of yours, from Portland. He was ever so pleased to find you. I told him you'd be here around noon, like usual." She smiled up at him. "And here you are."

Blake's head came up. "You–"

"He got here half an hour ago, actually. With another bloke. I knew you wouldn't mind, so I took them out to the boat." She smiled, her eyes blurred, missing Blake's horrified stare. "They were such nice lads, y'know – not like the scruffy lot you see today."

She brushed a stray hair off her forehead. "They must be awfully good mates to come up here to see you, all the way from Canberra," she said with a sly smile. "I saw the

7

airline tag on one of their bags, y'know? Had your picture, too. They was ever so pleased, like I say."

Blake set his beer down. He felt the heat suddenly, in a rush. Somewhere beyond the trees the dog still barked faintly over the drone of the insects, and from the jacarandas came the mirthless laughter of a kookaburra. Its mocking call followed him slowly back down the dock to where he had moored the workboat.

\* \* \*

"Welcome aboard, Blake. Come on down; we're in the forward cabin."

Blake came down the ladder from the deck warily, looking at the two young men seated at the small table in the center of the boat's cabin. One blond, one dark. Young, clean-cut, and well-dressed, with eyes that flicked into the corners and around the cabin, never still.

The dark one had curly hair and a neat moustache; the blond had bright blue eyes above a toothpaste smile. They could have been selling Bibles or cookware door-to-door except for the faint aura of controlled violence surrounding them. Blake reached the bottom of the ladder and stood, very still, watching them.

"Sit down, Blake," said the blond after a moment. He spoke with the easy authority of a cop. "Let's talk."

"I'll stand," said Blake evenly, moving his eyes around the Laurabada's small cabin. They'd done a professional job of searching, he saw. His few possessions were spread out across the bunk, the contents of his desk dumped on the deck. "What the hell's going on here? Who are you guys?"

The dark one laughed. "We're not cops, if that's what's worrying you." He smiled. "That's in a manner of speaking, of course. They call me Spike." He pointed to the blond one. "He's Max." He reached into his pocket and drew out a piece of paper. Unfolding it, he showed it to Blake. "And this, I believe, is you."

Blake's blood froze as he recognized himself in the photocopied clipping from *The Oregonian*, under the headline 'FBI seeks fugitive environmental terrorist'. Blake's eyes flicked to the desk drawer, broken open and lying on the deck.

Max smiled and held up his passport. "Looking for this?"

Blake took a step forward, reaching for the passport. Max drew back. "Relax, man, and listen to what we've got to say."

"To hell with that," Blake growled. "I want—"

Max nodded at Spike, who stood up, took one step forward and drove his fist into Blake's stomach. Expertly and hard. Blake crashed back against the bulkhead and sank to his knees, gasping.

Spike carefully hiked up his trousers and knelt down until his face was inches from Blake's. "The man said 'listen'. You got to pay attention when people talk to you, Blake. You ready to listen now?" He grabbed Blake's hair and yanked his head back. "Are you?"

Blake nodded.

Max unfolded himself from the chair and walked over to where Blake lay, doubled over. His eyes twinkled as he bent close. "Here it is, then. We know who you are, Blake. We know about Portland and about all the shit that went down there. We know what you did, we know where you've been. You're in trouble, my friend, but I guess you know that by now, right?"

Spike gave Blake's hair a savage twist. "Right?"

Blake nodded again. Something's terribly wrong here, he thought. In the past few years, he'd played a hundred scenarios through his head, but none of them went like this. It wasn't supposed to be happening this way at all.

"What do you want?" he whispered after a moment. "What the hell do you want?"

"Ah, now we're getting somewhere." Spike let go of his hair and stood up. "We want to take you for a ride. Our boss is over at the hotel, and he wants to talk to you." He dragged Blake to his feet. "Let's go. We're on kind of a deadline here."

"Hotel? I thought you guys worked out of the embassy."

Spike laughed. "We're not FBI, Blake. Not even close. And it's not a diplomatic reception you're being invited to. Now get a fucking move on, okay?"

# CHAPTER TWO

An overweight, balding man in shirtsleeves and a cigar stood with his back to them, staring out the picture window as they entered the suite at the hotel. In the background, the air conditioning roared softly. The man spoke without moving. "Any problems?"

Max and Spike shook their heads. "No, Mr. Sanford," they said in unison.

"Good. Go find Jeffries and get him in here. Then you boys take the afternoon off."

They nodded and melted back out the door.

The man turned around now, and looked at Blake, measuring him with careful eyes.

"I'm Amos Sanford," he said after a moment. "I run this little outfit here. Glad you could come."

Blake stood quietly, his hands loose at his sides, checking everything out carefully. Sanford looked to be somewhere in his late fifties, with heavy, black-rimmed glasses and an accent out of north Georgia, sounding as if he were carrying several little marbles around in his mouth. He seemed not to have shaved in the past week or so, and carried a paunch which sagged over the wide belt on his baggy trousers.

He looks like an irritable badger, Blake thought. His stomach was still sore from where Spike had hit him. "I didn't really have plans for the afternoon," he said drily.

11

Sanford's eyebrows lowered. "Don't be a smartass, son." He turned, pointing out the window with his cigar. "Say, what the fuck's that thing over there, in front of that big ugly building? Looks like a freeway or something. Except I didn't think they'd even have any freeways in this goddamn country."

"It's not a freeway," said Blake. "That's Parliament Road. It runs over from Waigani to the Parliament Building."

The view from the fifth-floor suite overlooked a wide four-lane road, virtually devoid of traffic. It led directly to the Parliament Building, an impressive structure with a soaring, pointed roof, overhanging brightly painted murals and sculptures.

"Doesn't look much like a parliament to me," grunted Sanford.

"It's meant to resemble a *haus tambaran* from the Sepik Province," said Blake. "It's a kind of traditional spirit house."

Sanford grinned. "Where the head cannibal works, huh?"

The door opened behind them and a man came in, a tan file folder in his hand.

"This is Ed Jeffries," said Sanford, glancing from the new man to Blake. "Don't try to bullshit him. Ed knows almost as much about you as I do."

Jeffries had a hard expression and pale eyes which inspected Blake without warmth. In his early forties, Blake guessed – he'd probably been a swimmer or tennis player at one time. With a big frame like that, he'd have to exercise to keep from getting fat. Jeffries sported fashionably cut, blow-dried hair, but he looked like he could take care of himself very well indeed.

I don't know what's going on here, Blake thought, or who these guys are, but this isn't the time to start trouble. I need to find out exactly what they know about me, and what they're planning. In the meantime, he told himself, keep your mouth shut and your fists at your sides.

Jeffries passed the file to Sanford, who sat down at the desk, opened it and began to leaf through its contents, puffing slowly on his cigar as he did so.

"Says here, Blake – and by the way, we know that's not your real name – that you got through nearly two years of graduate school before you fucked up."

Blake made no response.

Sanford looked up, adjusting his glasses. "That being the case, I'll assume you're a reasonably intelligent human being. Did the boys explain anything to you on the way over?"

Blake shook his head. "All I know is you're not the government."

Sanford chuckled then. "No, Mr. Blake, that we most surely are not. We're not any kind of government office, if that's what you're worried about. I run a little private firm. I'm in the information business, you might say." He pronounced it 'bid-ness'.

"Let me explain that just a little bit," Sanford continued, "before we get to what we want to talk to you about. I said I'm in the information business. It's a good business, and do you know why? Information is probably more valuable these days than gold or diamonds. But information is kinda unevenly distributed around the world. And that's how my little outfit makes its money."

He put his cigar down in the ashtray and leaned toward Blake. "Some people know things that other people don't, and that can sometimes be worth a lot. The intelligence boys – the CIA and those kinds of folks – are in it for politics, but we're not." He grinned. "Nope, just the money."

He sat back. "It's a very simple business model, you see. We find information that one party wants to keep secret, and we steal it. And then we sell it to somebody else. For as much money as we can. You with me so far?"

Blake nodded.

"And we're pretty damned good at it, if I say so myself. I started out as a lawyer, originally. Did a dozen years in corporate, working in translational research, and then another dozen in the university sector doing pretty much the same thing. It all boiled down to figuring out how to turn ideas into cash."

He smiled. "But here's the thing. Folks that come up with a good idea, something they can make money from, are generally shit-scared that somebody else will come along and steal it. They're usually dead right about that, as a matter of fact. And who better to do the stealing than someone who's been inside the operation for years?

"I sat and watched as other people got rich from information they'd paid pennies for, stuff that their research scientists or faculty guys had spent years coming up with. And when I was ready, I quit my job and went into business for myself. I knew where the good stuff was, and I knew how to find it." He paused. "That's how we found you, in fact. Ed here was with the FBI for some years, and then he went solo, as a bounty hunter. Now he works for me. His skills are kinda transferable, you might say."

Sanford flipped through the file.

"Though I have to say we stumbled on you more or less by chance. We went looking for a trail guide, your name came up in a search. Then we turned up a picture, and Ed thought he recognized you from somewhere."

"My picture?"

Jeffries spoke. "Wasn't hard at all, Blake, once we'd identified you. Everybody's got a cellphone these days. Your trekking buddies like to take pictures and post them online. Some of those pictures included you. It rang a bell from my FBI days. I matched the online shots to the Portland newspaper photo, and there we were." He snorted. "Pretty damn stupid, if you ask me, for someone trying to run from the law."

"On the other hand," Sanford said, "I don't blame you for running, son. You messed up bigly, I gotta say. You're wanted for half a dozen things, by the state of Oregon and the federal government. Arson, domestic terrorism, destruction of state and corporate property, aggravated assault, conspiracy. My, my. Only good thing is, you didn't kill anyone. Put a couple of folks in the hospital, though." He squinted at Blake through a cloud of cigar smoke. "You were an environmental activist that got a little too over-active."

"It was all a mistake," Blake said, thinking back to his involvement with the environmental protestors, and their attempt to sabotage the power plant. "None of us thought the whole place would go up like that. All we wanted to do was disable the equipment. I've always regretted how all that turned out."

Sanford snorted. "Sorry don't count for shit, son."

Blake took a breath. "So what happens now? You going to take me back to the States, collect some sort of reward or something?"

Sanford shook his head. "FBI and the State of Oregon want you, son; not us. Let 'em take care of their own damn business. Oh, hell no. Besides, I doubt your market value's that high back home. No, we got something else in mind, something much better." He plucked his cigar out of his mouth and inspected the ash. "And I'll get to that in a minute."

He stared out the window again, out beyond the streets and buildings of Waigani, up to the foothills of the jungle ranges rising behind the city.

"I can see why you'd wind up in a place like this," he said thoughtfully after a moment. "Most of stateside law enforcement's never heard of this country, couldn't find it on a map to save their lives. But how the hell do you make a living out here?"

Blake shrugged. "I do underwater photography – coral, shells and fish. I also collect some of the poisonous shells and sell them to medical researchers. In the dry season, I take trekking groups up into the bush."

"Tell me about the trekking business," Sanford said.

"Pretty straightforward, for the most part. The Aussies like to go up the Kokoda Trail, look at war relics; easy stuff like that. Once in a while there are folks that want to go further, into the ranges. I'll take them up into the Owen Stanleys or the Schraders for a few days. And every now and then, we'll get a group of biologists or plant people going to some out-of-the-way place, looking for specimens. Why?"

"You got equipment to do this sort of thing – tents and stuff?"

"Sure," said Blake. "I keep a bunch of equipment back on the boat, enough for a party of seven or eight."

"Do any rock climbing out here?"

There was a pause while Blake seemed to collect his thoughts. Then he said in a quiet voice, "I gave up rock work for a time. But once in a while some of my clients wanted to try some of the easier climbs, and eventually I gave in. I needed the money. I've got all the gear – ropes, pitons, all that." He looked at Sanford. "It's no big deal. I'll ask again – why?"

Sanford chuckled. "No big deal, he says. But it used to be, didn't it? A big deal, I mean. You used to be a pretty good climber, didn't you, Blake? According to what Jeffries here turned up."

Blake stared at him. "Jesus, man, that was a few years ago. Where the hell'd you get that information?"

Sanford glanced down at the papers in his file. "According to what Ed found out, you were an expert – won awards and everything. You worked summers as a professional guide in the Rockies, and you got picked for the US expedition to the Andes in your first year at graduate school. You didn't go." He looked at Blake, his eyes flat and curious. "Why not?"

Blake stood quietly as his mind went back to the Tetons, that afternoon on the high face, and the sudden freak storm that had coated the rock with ice. Once again, as he had so many times, he saw Becky's face as the piton ripped free and she began to fall. Heard her cry as she plunged four hundred feet straight down. The search party had found her thirty-six hours later, wedged into a crevice, bones shattered in a hundred places. He overheard one medic say she'd probably been alive all night, dying only toward dawn.

"Hey, man. He asked you a question." Jeffries moved in close beside him, his voice breaking the trance.

Blake's eyes came back into focus. "There was a climbing accident," he said slowly. "A– a friend of mine fell and died. That's why I stopped rock climbing for a time. Didn't care for it all that much." He paused. "The accident was my fault, you see."

Jeffries laughed harshly. "Jesus, what a fuck-up." He turned to Sanford. "If you ask me, this guy's no good, Amos. He's lost his nerve. I don't think–"

Blake's fist slammed into Jeffries' stomach, doubling the man over as a rush of air exploded from his lungs. A second later he crashed to the floor, gagging weakly.

White-faced, Blake stood over him, fists clenched. "She was my fiancée," he said with quiet fury. "Get up, you son of a bitch. I'm not finished."

Sanford put his hand on Blake's shoulder.

"Move back away now, son," he said with quiet authority. His grip was surprisingly hard. "He had it coming to him, but that's enough right now." To Jeffries he said, "Ed, get yourself up off that floor, hear? You look like five kinds of a damn fool lying there."

Blake stepped back warily as Jeffries came up off the floor, one hand on his stomach, his eyes on Blake. There's no mistaking his look, Blake thought. This man is vain and willful, and I've just humiliated him in front of his boss.

He is now my enemy. Whatever happens from now on, I'll have to watch this one. Every minute.

He turned to Sanford. "Look, what the hell is going on here? What do you want with me? You say you're not the law. You're not interested in sending me back. But you turn up on my goddamn boat and... and basically kidnap me. So, what's going on?"

Sanford shook his head. "We're not gonna send you back, son," he said quietly. "We're gonna make you a deal. Here," he said, gesturing to the table in front of him. "Sit down right here and let me explain some things to you."

With a baleful glance at Jeffries, Blake pulled out a chair and sat. "Anytime you're ready," he said.

Sanford frowned. "I told you before, son, don't be a smartass. I'm sorry we had to grab you off your boat like that, but we don't have a lot of time to waste here. Like I said, I'm in the information business. A few of days ago, we found out about a business opportunity, something that was just too good to ignore. We just gotta move a couple of the last pieces into place, and everybody stands to make a whole lot of money. Including you, if you behave yourself."

He picked up his cigar, stared at it fondly for a moment, and put it back in the ashtray. "We run this business on spec, see. Everybody pitches in, and when we score, everybody shares." He pointed a stubby finger at Blake. "Even you. Help us with what we got going here, and you'll make enough money to buy yourself a new life, anywhere you like. Hell, you could even stay here for all I care. How's that sound?"

Blake stared at him for a long moment. "What would I have to do?" he said quietly.

Sanford smiled. "Now we're getting to it." He cleared his throat. "We want you to help us find something. Do you know who Boomer Barrett is?"

"Everyone's heard of Barrett," said Blake. "He's one of the ten richest guys in the world, and a technology genius. Is that who you guys are really working for?"

Sanford gave a short bark of laughter. "Oh, no, Mr. Blake, we most definitely do not work for Boomer." He paused. "But we're involved with him, you might say."

Blake shook his head. "I don't understand."

"Mr. Boomer Barrett – and where he got that stupid name, I have no idea. His real name's Elmo, so what the hell, maybe it makes sense. He's a skinny little geeky guy, and he wants to look strong. All it does is make him look like a damned fool, if you ask me."

He shook his head.

"Sorry, got a little off track there. Anyway, our buddy Boomer has got his fingers in an awful lot of stuff, but right now, he's mainly interested in two things: computers, and space satellites. And so are we.

"Barrett is rich as Midas, but like most rich men, he wants to get even richer. This company he's got, the one called Envision has been developing a new kind of satellite, something he calls SkyScan. It's got a software system that can locate mineral deposits just by flying overhead. Kind of amazing, dontcha think?"

Blake shrugged. "Barrett's going into the mining business. So what?"

Sanford chuckled. "No, son. Barrett is in the information business, just like us. His intention is to use his SkyScan to map key parts of the earth's surface. The satellite will identify valuable mineral deposits and pinpoint their location. He's gonna map all that out, and then turn around and sell that information to various governments and private companies. And he's gonna make a shitload of money doing it."

Blake's eyes widened. "And you–"

Sanford grinned sharkishly, exposing large yellow teeth. "We're gonna fuck him up, boy, that's what." He gestured to Jeffries. "Ed, come on over here and sit down, join us while I explain a little more to our friend Blake."

Jeffries took a seat. Sanford got his cigar going again, and then began to speak.

"So, this new satellite of Barrett's, this SkyScan contraption, has been in development for about five years. Two months ago, it was finally finished. One week ago exactly, he sent it up, launched it from his own private site out in West Texas. Launch went fine, everything worked perfectly. The satellite made a few passes while they checked out systems and such, and then they turned on the scanner and began recording data. Two orbits later, something happened."

"It blew up?"

"No, it fell down. Or rather, it was brought down. And before it did, it sent a signal that it had found something. Mineral deposits, really valuable ones. Somewhere around here."

"You said the satellite was brought down?"

"We'll get to that in a minute, son. The SkyScan nose cone came down in some mountains west of here." He paused. "So now we're in kind of a hurry to find it before somebody else does. That nose cone's battery is broadcasting its position right now, and we need to get to it before the thing runs out of juice."

Blake looked at them. "And?"

"We want you to lead a party up into the ranges, Blake. Find the nose cone. Inside the nose cone there's a data module, and that's the piece we need to get our hands on." He examined the end of his cigar carefully. "We need to do that without attracting a whole lot of attention." He turned back to face Blake. "And we need to get it done real fast, before anyone else finds the damned thing."

Blake eyed him warily. "Where exactly do you think this nose cone is? And why do you think I'd be able to help you?"

"You'll see in a second." Sanford turned to Jeffries. "Ed, get me that map out of the desk over there."

Jeffries brought over a large topographic map, which Sanford unfolded and spread out across the tabletop.

Sanford stabbed his finger at a spot near the source of the Sepik River, at the very edge of the map. "We think it's somewhere around here. We want you to take us there."

Blake leaned forward. "Holy shit," he said softly after a moment. "You're talking about the Star Mountains. Some of these peaks are fifteen thousand feet high. Most of them aren't even in Papua New Guinea. They're across the border in Indonesian territory." He looked up. "Nobody goes over there, ever."

Sanford smiled. "You see the problem, then. We need somebody who knows the mountains. Somebody who can get us up in there and out again. Somebody who'll keep his mouth shut in the process."

Blake was shaking his head. "Do you have any idea what it will take to get a group up into that area? I mean—"

Sanford cut him off with an impatient wave. "We brought along more maps for you to look at, air photos, satellite – the whole nine yards. You'll also have help from the team, of course. There's a satellite technician and a data analyst waiting for us in Mount Hagen. Those two plus yourself as guide. And Ed, of course. Ed here's had a lot of experience outdoors."

Blake glanced at Jeffries. "I guess I understand the technician and the data guy. But what's *his* job?"

Jeffries returned his stare. "My job is keeping an eye on you, Blake. Just in case you get any ideas." He smiled tightly. "I'll be watching you the whole time. You mess up – just once – and I'll finish what we started here. I'll look forward to it, in fact."

Sanford tapped his cigar impatiently. "Well, son? You in or out? Like I said, we work on a profit-sharing basis in this outfit. You'll get a share of whatever we make off this little caper." He paused. "Otherwise, it'll be a phone call to the authorities back in the States."

Blake looked again at the map. Sanford watched him carefully. Finally, Blake sighed. "I don't really have a choice, do I?"

Sanford chuckled, a dry sound like leaves on asphalt.

"I like a sense of humor in a man," he said. "Spike and Max'll take you back to your boat. Collect whatever equipment you'll need and be back here in an hour. We're flying up to the Highlands this afternoon. The rest of the team's already there, waiting for us."

# CHAPTER THREE

They sat huddled around a large table in a corner of the dining room at the Kimininga Lodge in Mount Hagen, all of them wearing sweaters and light jackets against the chill of the Highlands night. Maps, sketches, open laptops and aerial photographs littered the table. The group were the only guests in the Lodge, and the staff had been given instructions to leave them strictly alone.

Blake, Sanford and Jeffries had come up from Port Moresby that afternoon, leaving Spike and Max behind. They flew in a commercial Air Niugini Dash-8 aircraft, a bumpy two-hour ride along the flanks of the Owen Stanleys, up into the Bismarck Range, finally coming down through mist and cloud into the Waghi Valley and a smooth landing at Hagen's Kagamuga Airport. They had stepped out of the plane into crisp, cool air scented with woodsmoke.

Jeffries looked around approvingly. "Nice change from the heat down on the coast," he said. "And look at those mountains."

Blake snorted. "Those aren't mountains, Jeffries. They're hills. Wait till you see where we're going."

Carrying his heavy briefcase, Sanford climbed down the aircraft stairs, puffing and grunting. "You two can admire the scenery later," he said. "Go make sure we've got all the equipment, and then let's get over to the Lodge, meet the others."

The Kimininga Lodge lay just off the road to the airport, several miles from the town center. Sanford had booked bungalows away from the main reception area, and once they'd checked and stowed the climbing equipment, he'd ordered Blake and Jeffries into the dining room for a planning meeting. There, they'd been met by the two other members of the party, and Blake's earlier misgivings intensified.

One of them was clearly an alcoholic. The other – equally clearly – was a woman.

Ray Corley, introduced as a specialist in satellite software design, looked to be in his mid-forties, and in mediocre physical condition, at best. He'd had a big glass of whiskey in his hand when Blake walked into the room, and now, just before nine o'clock, he'd managed to down two more. His thick glasses and puffy cheeks gave him the appearance of a radio-era whiz kid. Ill at ease, his eyes darted around the room, the tip of his pink tongue licking his fleshy lips between sips from his whiskey glass. He wore baggy trousers and a frayed white shirt, and Blake would bet he'd never run a mile in his life.

Jill Winters was quite a different matter. Sanford had introduced her as a data encryption specialist and a trained nurse, which seemed to Blake to be a very unlikely combination. He guessed her to be in her early thirties, and decided that 'striking' was the only word that really fit her appearance. Tall and slim, she wore her jet-black hair in a no-nonsense ponytail under a faded Caltech ball cap, the way a runner would. Her down vest set off her trim, athletic figure. He found himself drawn again and again to her eyes – large and green, with irises like fractured glass. Yes, he thought, definitely striking.

Sanford lit a fresh cigar, puffed it experimentally a few times, and called the meeting to order. "Let's get going," he said. "I've already briefed Blake here about our little problem. SkyScan fell out of orbit two days ago and landed somewhere west of here in what Blake says are the Star

Mountains. We need a professional to get us up into there, and Blake got picked. Now we've gotta find the damned thing before anybody else does."

Blake spoke up. "Who else actually knows about this?"

Sanford snorted. "Well, Boomer Barrett sure as hell does. And if he does, I'm betting that some of his competitors in Asia and Europe do, too."

"How would they even find out?" Blake asked.

Jill Winters gave him a tight smile. "There's really no such thing as secure communication these days, Mr. Blake. All it would take is someone intercepting an internal office memo."

Sanford broke in. "Or anybody who's monitoring satellite activity closely – NASA, the Russians, even the Indonesians, if they were on the ball. So we need to get there first."

Ray Corley looked up from his drink. "There's another reason we need to locate it before anyone else does. That nose cone's got a self-destruct mechanism. I designed it myself. It blows everything to hell if somebody tampers with it." His voice had gone blurry around the edges.

"So it'll be useless junk if the Indonesians get hold of it. It's possible, even likely, that other people know that Barrett's satellite is offline. But we're the only people – so far – who know where," said Sanford.

"Not for long," said Corley. "It will occur to somebody to run the numbers on where its orbit began to decay. And that might tell them where it's likely to have come down. It'll probably take them a while, but we need to sneak in and get it before anybody notices."

"Finders keepers, in other words," Blake said drily. "But you said before that the satellite had been brought down deliberately. So presumably whoever did that also knows."

Corley grinned then, looking like a little kid. "We brought it down, Blake. Or rather, I did."

Blake stared at him. "You did? How?"

Sanford leaned forward. "Remember a few years ago what a big deal it was when Boomer figured out how to bring one of his rockets back down onto a floating platform? Remember what a neat trick that was? Well, Boomer didn't do that – Ray here did. He designed the software system to bring that baby down onto a dime, and in one piece." He took a puff of his cigar. "And that's what Ray did with this one."

Jeffries gave a derisive snort. "Except that he kinda fucked it up, didn't he? It wasn't supposed to come down in the mountains. Ray here was probably operating under a little too much Jack Daniel's that day."

"Fuck you, Ed. I got it down, didn't I?" Corley said. "And I got the beacon's frequency changed so they can't track it."

"They'll figure that one out soon enough, though, won't they?" said Jeffries.

"Shut up, the both of you." Sanford's voice broke into the argument. He leaned forward and addressed Blake. "You've been going over those maps and pictures all evening. Got anything figured out yet?"

Blake pushed the large topographic map out into the center of the table. "None of you have climbed before," he said. "And none of you are really in condition for what you're about to do. The Stars are one of the most remote and rugged mountain ranges on the island. I don't–"

"Spare us, Blake," growled Jeffries from the end of the table. "Nobody gives a shit about any of that. Your job is to tell us how to find the goddamned thing, and then take us up to get it. Move it along, will you?"

"Just so we all understand the situation," Blake said evenly. "Our chances of coming back with what we're looking for aren't very good." He looked around the table. Everyone was quiet now. "And you need to know the reasons why."

He put his finger on a spot on the map. "First, if that nose cone is where you think it is, it's up at around thirteen thousand feet, in one of the most remote parts of the island. None of us will be acclimatized for that altitude. We're likely to get sick, in other words. Second, we'll be using ropes and pitons for at least part of the trip. None of you have ever done that. With inexperienced people, roped climbing can be very dangerous. Third, it's the monsoon season on this part of the island. That means rain every day, lots of mud, lots of insects. The rivers will be full, the currents swift, and there'll be dense cloud most of the time on top of the ridges."

Jeffries rolled his eyes. "Jesus, you're Mr. Good News himself, aren't you? Anything else you want to tell us?"

"As a matter of fact, yes. If this nose cone is where you think it is, we'll have to cross the Indonesian border to get to it."

"You mean we have to have visas?" Corley asked.

Jeffries snorted. "No, you dumb–"

Blake cut him off. "It's a legitimate question. But no. No visas. This" – he pointed on the map – "is what used to be called Irian Jaya. It's now called Papua Barat – West Papua. Where we're going is in an administrative area they call Pegunungan Bintang – Star Mountains District."

"So you've been there before?" Sanford asked.

Blake gave a tight smile. "Oh, hell no," he said. "In fact, I don't know anyone who's been up into the Stars that far. There were some early expeditions, Dutch and Australian, years ago, but since independence, that whole area is pretty restricted. Nobody goes in there."

"What happens if we get caught?"

Blake shook his head. "Nothing good. Getting arrested would probably be the nicest thing that would happen. We're going to have to make sure that it doesn't. The Indonesians have a hair trigger where that area is concerned, and they don't like intruders. They're fighting a low-intensity jungle war with the Papua Merdeka Movement these days, and they'll have patrols all over the border areas."

Jill Winters furrowed her brow. "What's Papua Merdeka?"

"The Free Papua Movement. When the Indonesians took over the island from the Dutch, they faced pushback from the local tribes. It's been going on for years. First it was spears and axes, but now some of the locals have got guns. They've managed to kill quite a few people over time."

Sanford set his cigar down carefully in the ashtray. "So if you get in trouble, you can't call for help. Okay, Blake, we've all heard the bad news. Now tell us how you're gonna get these folks in there."

"According to the coordinates you gave me, this thing's somewhere up on the side of Mount Antares, about five miles across the border."

"Antares," said Winters. "The rival of Mars, god of war." She looked around at their expressions and grinned. "World Mythology class as an undergraduate. I'm not just a data engineer, you know. Are all the mountains named after stars?"

"Most of them. The Stars form a chain running west from the Hindenburg Range inside Papua New Guinea, across the border into Indonesia. First there's Capella and Scorpio, then Antares. Further west are Andromeda and Betelgeuse."

Jeffries peered at the map. "Can you be a little more specific about where the nose cone is?"

"Not yet," said Blake. "Once we get closer, if the signal's still being broadcast, we can get a better fix. Right now, the best I can tell from what you've given me is that it's somewhere on the approach ridge, up close to the top."

"Sonofabitch," breathed Sanford. "Okay, what's the next move?"

"Tomorrow morning," Blake said, "we charter a plane and go up toward the border. There's an airstrip here" – he tapped the map – "at a village called Wambip. That's as close as we can get. At that point, we'll be about fifteen miles from where the nose cone is."

"What happens then?" Sanford said.

"We start walking. Due west. There's a river we can follow for some of the way. There's probably a trail alongside it, but I can't be sure from the air photos."

"Well, what if there isn't a trail?" asked Ray Corley.

"Then we might as well turn around and come back," Blake answered. "We'd never be able to cut through fifteen miles of jungle. I'm optimistic, though. There are people living at Wambip, you can see their huts on the air photographs. And where there are people, there are trails.

"Wambip's at about five thousand feet. We follow the river due west up the valley for about eight miles, climbing up only a few hundred feet. That's the easy part. After that, we leave the river and cross into Indonesian territory. Once we leave the river, we have to get up a steep ridge, then through jungle and rainforest for about five miles. Once we do that, we'll come out on what looks like a flat grassy plateau, just below the main summit crest."

Jill Winters leaned forward. "That plateau – how high is it?"

"About ten thousand feet. Why?"

"Well, I can do the math. That's five thousand feet of altitude in five miles. A thousand feet up for each mile of trail. Isn't that going to be awfully difficult?"

Blake smiled tightly. "I didn't create the geography here, Ms. Winters. But yes, it's going to be difficult." He looked around at them. "If you want your electronic toy, you'll have to do it."

"Cut the shit," said Jeffries. "What happens next?"

"The air photographs and satellite images show the plateau as a nearly flat patch of short grass, what they call *kunai* here, a couple of miles across. At that point we're probably fairly close to where the nose cone is, so we'll set up a base camp there. We can rest there before we try the next step."

"Why don't we just keep going?" said Jeffries. "Christ, we're practically there. Isn't that what you just said?"

"It gets a lot harder from here on," said Blake. "That climb up the ridge to get to the *kunai* plateau is going to be difficult, but it's not complicated, and it's not particularly dangerous. This next part is both of those things."

"What do you mean?"

"Getting up to the summit ridge means going up this rock wall. It goes from the edge of the *kunai* straight up, to the central crest of the range. If we can get up to the crest, then it's another couple of miles to the summit of Antares. At that point, we're going to be about thirteen thousand feet up. That's where we'll find the nose cone." He paused. "If it's there."

Winters bent forward to look at the map, tracing the contour lines with her finger. "Is this the rock wall you're talking about? It looks steep."

"That's it. It's about two thousand feet high, and it looks to be pretty much straight up and down in places." He looked around the table. "And we've got to climb it."

Ray Corley put his drink down. "You mean with these ropes and spikes and things you brought? Jesus, can't we just go around the cliff or something?"

Blake shook his head. "There's no other way up to the crest. We've just got to make it, somehow."

"And from then on, it's clear sailing?" asked Jeffries.

Blake shook his head. "Probably not. Your nose cone is up there somewhere, but we won't know exactly where until we get closer."

"Blake's right. We'll need to triangulate on the signal before the nose cone batteries die. The closer we are, the better," said Winters.

Blake nodded. "That's when the last stage begins. We'll need to search along the crest."

"Jesus," muttered Corley, staring into his whiskey glass.

"The problem is that the crest itself is pretty much of a mystery," continued Blake. "The contour interval on the maps is too great to show detail, there's too much parallax distortion in the aerial photos, and the satellite views have a lot of cloud cover that obscures detail. The crest looks to be pretty sharp, and there's a deep glacial valley – a cirque of some kind – on the south side, just below Antares's summit. If the nose cone's somewhere on the crest we ought to spot its drag chute, but if it went down into the valley, we might never find it. According to the map, the cirque drops off more than three thousand feet in less than a third of a mile."

He turned to Ray Corley, who was shaking his head in disbelief. "That's partly why we have to go up the rock wall from the grassy plateau. All the other ways onto the crest are a lot worse."

Sanford grunted. "Shit fire," he said. "Got any other happy news for us?"

Blake shrugged. "That's about it. Once we reach the *kunai* plateau, we'll be above the treeline. That means bare rock, wind and freezing temperatures at night. And no people. The area's pretty much of a no man's land, really. It's so remote that I'm guessing nobody much goes in there. We're not likely to see people at all after we leave Wambip airstrip."

"Except maybe an Indonesian patrol," said Jeffries in a dry voice. "Okay. How long do you figure it'll take to get up to where the nose cone is?"

"If we were experienced and in condition, it might take two or three days. But we're not." Blake thought for a moment. "Say a week. Maybe more."

"No way," said Jeffries quietly. "We'll have to do it in less. The batteries in the transmitter won't last forever."

Blake folded the map carefully. "Let's get something straight," he said, his eyes flicking around the group. "I didn't ask for this job. But I know a few things about mountains, and one thing I know is that schedules and deadlines don't mean much up there. Enter the mountains and you're in a total environment where nothing works

31

quite the way it does at sea level. And to stay alive, you don't fight that environment, you accept it."

He spoke directly to Jeffries. "You can't negotiate a better deal with the mountains; you can't bully them."

The rest of the group watched him carefully.

"You're all untrained and out of condition for what we're about to attempt," Blake went on. "None of you have any idea of what you're getting into." He paused, feeling the heat rising in his cheeks. "You want to know what I think? I think we'll be damned lucky to walk out of there alive."

Winters flushed. Corley's gaze met his and slid away. Jeffries stared stonily at the map – his expression unreadable.

Winters got up. "I need some air," she said, walking away toward the outside terrace.

Everyone watched her go. Then Amos Sanford smiled and turned to Blake.

"You've made your point, son," he said. "But just remember one thing. If they don't make it, you don't make it. You keep that in mind, hear?" He looked at his watch. "It's late. Y'all have got a big day tomorrow. Time everybody went to bed."

Blake watched them collect their gear and shuffle off to their rooms, their expressions thoughtful and subdued. He sat by himself at the table, collecting the maps and photos, and thinking. He'd meant what he said to the group: you couldn't negotiate with a mountain. You couldn't change any of the basic equations. Time, distance, altitude; none of them would budge an inch. The human response was all that mattered, if getting out alive was your goal. Up on the mountain, he thought, it might come down to hard choices, to winners and losers.

And he intended to be a winner, whatever the cost.

As he headed to his room, he found Jill Winters outside, leaning on the rail, smoking a cigarette. The night air had turned cold, the stars were shining bright and steady. She threw the cigarette away when she saw him coming.

"I don't usually smoke," she said in an embarrassed voice. "Only when I'm stressed. And tonight–"

"Don't apologize," Blake said. "You've got a lot to think about."

She put her hand on his arm. "Tell me the truth," she said. "Is this going to work? Do we have any chance of doing this?"

He thought for a moment before replying.

"I really don't know," he said. "I take untrained groups into the mountains all the time. But not into places like this. We're going to have to be very, very careful, and we're going to have to trust one another; take care of each other."

She nodded. "I trust Ray. I worked with him for years. Jeffries – I just don't know. He seems, well, maybe relentless is the word I'm looking for."

Blake smiled at her then. "Don't worry about Jeffries," he said. "The mountain usually takes care of people like that... Otherwise, I'll take care of him myself." He turned. "You'd better get some sleep. Like Sanford said, big day tomorrow."

He felt her eyes watching him as he walked down the path to his bungalow.

\* \* \*

This is madness, he thought later as he lay on his sagging bed waiting for sleep to come. We're just asking for trouble, going up into the Stars with people like this. Jeffries is a macho hothead, plenty of muscle but no sense. Corley's practically boozeblind; he'll be lucky if he can carry his pack. And the woman – well, it was too early to tell about the woman.

It didn't matter anyway, he thought. Sooner or later, one of them would make a mistake. And the mountains don't give anyone second chances. There was safety in numbers, but only up to a point. Once a group began to break down under pressure, Blake knew from hard experience, numbers would become a liability. Like a chain, a climbing team was only as strong as its weakest link. Who would that weak link be, Blake wondered?

He turned over and listened for a moment to the night, thinking. Somewhere up on the mountain, the expedition might turn into an unplanned exercise in survival.

And he planned to be a survivor.

# CHAPTER FOUR

Blake rummaged in his pack in the chilly pre-dawn darkness beside the hangar. Patches of night fog still lay on the ground, but the stars over the Bismarck and Schrader Ranges to the northeast winked bright and cold. To the west, however, he saw that the stars were blotted out. The clouds must already be building, he thought.

He closed his rucksack and stood up. "We're pretty heavy," he announced. "We've got at least forty pounds each, not counting that electronic equipment of yours."

"That radio equipment's your ride back to civilization," Sanford said, hefting one of the rucksacks experimentally. "Once you get down from the mountain, Ray will call on the radio for us to come up and get you. And that reminds me, I need to collect your cellphones. Everybody's. I've already got Ed's. Now."

Jill Winters and Ray Corley, seated on a pile of gear, passed their phones to Blake. He added his and handed them to Sanford, who tucked them away into his briefcase. "Cellphones can be tracked," he explained. "We're running silent from now on."

Blake shrugged. "There's no cellphone service where we're going. But if it makes you feel better, fine."

He looked over at Winters and Corley. They were both staring at a group of Jiga tribesmen, dressed only in arse-grass and kina-shell necklaces, who had emerged from the darkness and now sat, squatting, ten feet away. They chewed betel nut silently, their eyes glowing in the faint light. From time to time one of them would pivot slowly and spit a thick stream of bright red juice onto the tarmac.

Corley looked sick, his face pale and sweaty. He's probably got a hangover, and no wonder.

It's bad enough, he thought, taking an untrained team into the ranges like this, but somebody not in complete control of himself is worse than a liability – he'd be a menace to everyone around him. And speaking of menaces, where the hell was Jeffries?

Blake pulled his pack straps tight, stood up, and went into the tiny office of the air charter company.

Inside, Jeffries leaned against the wooden counter, arguing with a bored young Australian in a dirty pilot's uniform. "I don't get it, friend," Jeffries was saying. "What the hell do you mean, 'no guarantees'? We're paying out good fucking money, aren't we?"

The Australian scratched at the end of his nose with a dirty fingernail. "Look, mate," he said patiently, "I've already explained it once. Take a dekko out the window there." He pointed to where clouds bulked low over the mountains to the west, just visible now in the pale dawn light. "That'll be rain in a little while up where you're going. Or not. Might just shoot through and come rain over here. But if I was to fly you up into that mess right now, you could very well be wasting your money. It could be pissing down up there for all I know. Probably is. And after a rain, the strips are usually too wet to land on. You'd get in all right, but we'd all stay there, cos the bloody plane would be stuck up to the prop in mud." He paused. "And believe me, that's not a place you want to get stuck."

"Can't you get some sort of a weather report from the village? Or something?" Jeffries said.

The pilot grinned, showing bad teeth. "The only way to know for sure what's going on up in those hills is to go on up and take a look. And if you do that, you pay the charter rate, no matter what happens."

Jeffries turned to Blake. "Jesus Christ," he said. "What the hell can you do with people like this?"

"Give him the money and let's go," Blake said quietly. "The weather's as good as it gets up here. In a few hours it will rain, and then we'll have to wait and try again tomorrow."

"Glad to see there's one smart bloke in yer mob, anyway," said the pilot from behind them. "Cash in advance, takeoff in ten minutes if you'll be so kind" – he winked – "and I'll carry yer cargo for free, seeing as how we're not even half full."

"Thanks," muttered Jeffries drily as he counted out bills and accepted a scrawled receipt. "Come on," he said, turning to Blake. "Let's get our damn junk loaded. I just want to get the hell out of here."

\* \* \*

The sun's disc edged up over the tarmac as the green and white Britten-Norman Islander nosed out of its hangar. It sat trembling at the edge of the runway for a moment, and then roared smoothly into the air.

The pilot put on his headset, popped a large wad of Juicy Fruit gum into his mouth, and signed off with Hagen Tower as he turned the aircraft west and began to climb away from the rising sun. The twin-engine craft bumped and swayed in the morning air currents as it clawed its way up to cruising altitude and began to plod steadily across the Western Highlands, toward the mist-shrouded land of the West Sepik Province.

Blake sat in the copilot's seat, listening to the Australian's voice crackling through the headset. "We've got about forty minutes of flying time to Wambip. We go past Mount Giluwe and Kandep, over Kopiago, and then straight west past Telefomin, with the Victor Emanuels to our north. We'll make one high pass over the strip to check it out. Then I'll either try and set her down or we'll abort and come back. Fair enough?"

Blake turned and shouted the information back to the others in the seats behind him. He got a curt nod from Jeffries in return. Corley's face had gone dead white – as white as his knuckles gripping the back of Blake's seat. Winters was in the rearmost seat, out of sight behind a small mountain of gear.

Blake settled back and gazed out the window at the dense green forest unrolling underneath them like a huge, uneven carpet. We've been in the air only ten short minutes, he thought, and already there's no further sign of civilization visible. Only the twisted red-earth scar of the Highlands Highway, crawling painfully into the rugged interior ranges, marked man's presence. Soon, he knew, even that would disappear as they moved further west, closer to the wild and remote border area.

The land turned steeper and more rugged now, covered with thick jungle except where the silver flash of a river or the white scar of an old avalanche broke through the dense green. Every few miles a native village appeared, a lonely collection of low huts perched on a ridgetop or huddled deep in the shadow of a valley. Between them, nothing but dense forest.

Patches of fog still nestled in some of the deeper valleys, not yet burnt away by the sun. The Islander skimmed along just above the ridges, banking slightly from left to right as the pilot followed the contours of the land west and into the foothills of the Victor Emanuel Range near Telefomin. Beyond the Emanuels, Blake knew, lay the Hindenburg Range.

And beyond the Hindenburgs, the Stars.

Unknown territory for me, Blake thought with a twinge of excitement mixed with a deeper anxiety. He had never ventured into the ranges beyond the Western and Southern Highlands areas; they were too remote and rugged, and even the hardiest trekkers and climbers preferred the established trails, the known routes.

Blake knew that aside from some mining in the Ok Tedi area, there was little human activity along the border. The region had remained sparsely settled, and what few people there were lived largely untouched by the outside world in all but the most superficial ways. Blake found himself wondering what it would be like to crash in this forbidding country – to have to find a way out of the forest and back to safety. Wondering what it would be like to be on his own down there.

"What's in Wambip, then?" he asked the pilot. "Do they have a patrol post there?"

The pilot's snort came through harshly on the earphones. "Patrol post? You're bloody dreaming, mate. They've got sweet bugger-all in Wambip – just a pack of hairy-assed locals living in grass huts."

The pilot popped his gum. "Shit of a place, really. The nearest radio is over with the government officer in Telefomin. About a week's walk, I'd reckon." He shot a glance at Blake. "You worried about getting out again, is that it?"

"It had occurred to me," said Blake drily.

The pilot grinned. "No worries. We fly a scheduled run up into Wambip every Sunday when the weather's decent. You only missed the last one by a day. You could have got in here for a fraction of what you're paying on the charter rate. I didn't tell your mate that, though." He glanced sideways at Blake. "You, ah, in some kind of hurry, are you?"

"You could say that." Their cover story came easily to Blake's lips. "We're doing plant research, collecting samples of the local flora. We have to be back at the university soon."

The pilot chewed his gum, making popping noises in the earphones. "Yanks are always in a bloody hurry, near as I can make out," he said after a moment. "Collecting local flora, is it? Plenty of that about up here, no fucking doubt. The lads in the village will probably lend a hand if you pay 'em. They're decent enough, really – better behaved than most of the locals up here. Still lazy as buggery, though. Want money for everything."

He banked the plane expertly around a tall ridge and adjusted the throttles, changing the pitch of the propellers. "Coming up now," he murmured. "The moment of truth. Just ahead."

\* \* \*

Their first glimpse of Wambip was not impressive. They came in low over the settlement, the shadow of the Islander flickering over the cleared ground below. Blake counted twenty-odd huts clustered in the little clearing, wisps of smoke rising lazily from cooking fires. At the end of the village a tattered windsock marked the border of a long field of short grass which served as the landing strip.

The pilot looked satisfied and thumbed his mike button. "Golf Kilo Bravo to Hagen Tower. Wambip's clear – we're going in."

Without waiting for a reply, he put the Islander into a tight climbing turn, roaring close above the forested slopes overlooking the river.

"This one's a real pisser, my bloody oath it is," the pilot muttered. "Doesn't look like all that much, does it? But you only get one shot at the approach. No room to pull up and go round if something goes wrong."

Looking ahead, Blake understood what he meant. Beyond the village, the river valley narrowed sharply into a tight corridor, blocked abruptly at the far end by a steep ridge. That must be the way up, Blake thought; the ridge we have to climb to get to the grass plateau and the mountains beyond.

It loomed up like a massive wall over the tiny village, much steeper than it had seemed from the maps.

The Islander steadied now, settling into her approach, drifting down smoothly through wispy patches of mist. The pilot flipped switches and levers in sequence, trimming the flaps and cutting back the throttles. "Got to watch out for animals on the strip," he muttered. "Mate of mine had a prang last year on a landing just like this. Ran straight into a herd of bloody pigs, of all things."

He made last-second adjustments. "There, she's right now. Grab yer socks."

A thump, and water splashed up from the wheels on either side of the cockpit. The pilot gunned the motors hard, and the Islander bumped and lumbered reluctantly along the grass toward the small crowd of people that had somehow materialized at the end of the strip. The pilot made a tight turn, raced the motors one last time, and cut power.

The roaring in Blake's ears died, leaving only humid silence. The odor of woodsmoke and rotting vegetation invaded the cabin as the door flipped open.

"Welcome to Wambip," said the pilot, taking off his headset.

They clambered stiffly out the door and onto the soggy strip, blinking in the bright sunlight. Forty or fifty villagers stood behind a makeshift gate a few yards from the plane, staring silently at the newcomers. At the sight of Jill Winters, a ripple of excitement passed through the crowd.

Blake looked them over. There were roughly equal numbers of men, women, pigs and children. The men sported ragged shorts and faded T-shirts. Some of them carried bush knives and steel axes with long, tapered handles. The women wore faded mission dresses, some cradling small naked babies on their hips. They stared with open curiosity, unmoving, at the strangers.

Behind them, smoke rose from a cluster of decaying thatched huts on stilts. Dogs yapped in the distance, in counterpoint to the steady drone of flies from a nearby rubbish heap.

"Jesus," muttered Corley as he staggered out of the plane, his face drenched with sweat. "Excuse me, will ya?" He disappeared behind the tail section, out of sight.

Blake, Jeffries and Winters stood silently, taking in the scene. The waiting crowd stared back, their faces expectant, eyes gleaming with curiosity and excitement. They've come to see a play, Blake thought, and now the first act is about to begin. The house lights have dimmed, the curtain's rising, the actors have taken their places. Soon, the first lines will be spoken.

From somewhere behind him came the harsh sounds of Corley vomiting up his breakfast onto the grass.

Jeffries shook his head and spat on the ground. "Right, let's get the goddamn gear out," he said.

# CHAPTER FIVE

Jill Winters stood at the end of the airstrip watching the receding dot of the Islander, on its way back to Mount Hagen. She turned, brushing hair back from her forehead. "There it goes, Peter. Our last link with the outside." She swung around, staring up the valley. "This is amazing, isn't it? It's like something out of *King Kong*."

Blake followed her gaze up the massive ridge which dominated the valley behind the village. It stretched completely across the horizon to the west, topped by a heavy cloud blanket which spilled across the top and down the sides. By early afternoon, Blake knew, the clouds would cover the valley floor, and it would begin to rain.

"That huge ridge, blocking everything off," Winters said in a low voice. "God. You almost expect to see dinosaurs flying around up there."

"It's almost five thousand feet high – you can't even see the top of it from here." Blake indicated the crowd of villagers standing off to the side of the airstrip. "Excuse me a moment."

Blake walked over and stood in front of them. "*Moning tru, olgeta,*" he spoke in a loud, confident voice. He received cautious nods and murmurs in return. He raised his voice a notch or two. "*Igat sampela man long hap hia i save tok inglis?*"

Jeffries came up beside Winters. "What the hell's he doing?"

"He's getting us guides and carriers, Ed," she said. "You didn't think we were going to be able to haul all this up the mountain by ourselves, did you?"

Jeffries grunted and walked back to where Corley stood, picking through their pile of gear.

Winters watched as Blake talked quietly and intensely in Pidgin with the waiting crowd. Finally, he walked back to join her, followed by two of the villagers.

"I've been talking to these two," he said. "They say there's a hunting trail which will take us up to the plateau."

The two men in question stood behind Blake, staring with frank curiosity at the pile of gear. The younger one, tall and slim, wore faded shorts and a checked shirt. The older man had skin the color and texture of saddle leather. He wore a Salvation Army bandmaster's cap, and was smoking a foot-long cigarette made from rolled newspaper. Both men had broad, lined faces and quick, intelligent eyes. Neither one wore shoes.

"This is Imea," Blake said, indicating the younger of the two. "He speaks English."

"How do you do?" said Imea gravely.

"And this is the village headman."

The old man grinned, showing a mouthful of crooked teeth stained black by a lifetime's betel chewing.

"Let's go get the others," said Blake. "The sooner we get started, the better."

"Ed and Ray are over there," Winters said, dropping her voice. "There's some trouble, I think."

Jeffries rose as they approached. In his hand, he held a full bottle of whiskey out to them. "Look at this, for Christ's sake," he snapped. "He was just getting it out of his pack." He turned to Corley, sitting miserably on the ground. "You goddamn fool," he spat.

Corley's hands trembled as he struggled to light a cigarette. "For Christ's sake, Ed," he muttered. "It's only a bottle of whiskey. Okay, so I had a few drinks last night. Is that a crime?"

"It is if you make yourself so sick you can't function. Look at you – you've just puked your guts up." Jeffries wiggled the bottle. "This goes in the river, right now!"

"Wait." Blake moved forward, taking the bottle from his hand. "Don't throw it away. We may need it later on." He had caught the look of panic on Corley's face. Whether or not the man's an alcoholic, he's nervous as hell about something, Blake thought. If a couple of drinks a day will hold him together, it's worth the extra weight.

Jeffries glared at him for a moment. Then he shrugged. "Whatever you say, hotshot. But it goes in your pack, got it? Don't let Ray near the stuff." He caught sight of Imea and the headman. "And who the fuck are these guys?"

"The local welcoming committee," said Blake. "They say we can go straight up the valley, following the river, and then turn northwest to get up onto the ridge." He walked over to one of the packs and opened it, pulling out a money belt and several cartons of cigarettes.

"Hey, that's my rucksack," said Jeffries. "What the hell do you think you're doing?"

Blake turned around. "We need to negotiate for guides," he said. "So, with all due respect, I'd like everybody to sit down now and shut the fuck up."

"But–"

Winters laid a hand on Jeffries' shoulder. "Do as he says, Ed."

When everyone was seated, Blake laid the money belt and the cigarette cartons on the grass in front of him. "Now listen to me carefully," he said to Imea, "and then tell him exactly what I say. Understand?"

Imea nodded.

Blake ripped open the cigarette cartons one by one and spread the packs on the ground. Then he unzipped the money belt and took out a thick wad of bills. The headman spat red betel juice and watched carefully, his eyes bright. Leaving the women behind, the rest of the village men edged forward, moving in closer, staring at the money and the cigarettes with barely concealed excitement.

"We want to go up the trail to the *kunai* plateau. Right now, today. Tell him that."

An excited whisper spread through the crowd as Imea translated.

"Tell him we want three strong men with us. Only three, but they have to be strong." He pointed to the packs. "They'll carry most of the equipment."

As he spoke, Blake separated kina banknotes from the wad and spread them out in four piles where everyone could see them. He put two packs of cigarettes beside each pile.

"Each man will get these cigarettes and this money for agreeing to go with us." He reached into the money belt and drew out more notes. "Every day, each man will get this much more." He added money and cigarettes to the piles in front of him.

The crowd watched, whispering excitedly among themselves.

Blake swept his arm up toward the ridge behind him. "If we reach the plateau in two days or less, each man will get double this." He paused while Imea translated. He heaped more bills on top of the cigarette packs. "Once we reach the plateau, the men can come back to the village by themselves." He looked at the headman. "Ask him if there are any questions."

Imea and the headman talked quietly for a moment. Then Imea addressed Blake. "He says that the *kunai* plateau is across the border. That it is dangerous to cross the border. He asks why you wish to do this dangerous thing."

He can ask, Blake thought, but I'm not going to answer. Instead, he pulled more bills from his roll. "Tell him," he said, keeping his eyes on the headman, "that we need to leave within the hour – no later. Those who go with us will get all this" – he indicated three of the piles –

"and the headman gets this." Slowly, he added more bills to the fourth pile. "And he keeps his questions to himself." He sat back on his heels. "Ask him if he understands."

As Imea translated, Blake could feel the crowd beginning to relax. The men began to smile and laugh among themselves. After a few moments, the headman roared for silence, spoke a few staccato phrases to Imea, and began to scoop up the money.

"He agrees," said Imea. "Myself and two of the best hunters in the village. We can leave now. But," he added, his dark face serious, "he does not think you will reach the *kunai* in two days. White men are strong in their heads, he says, but not in their legs." He pointed to Corley. "This one, he says, is weak. He should not go."

Ed Jeffries stood up. "We all go. Including Ray here. Even if I have to drag him every step of the fuckin' way. Tea party's over, Blake. Let's get the show on the road."

* * *

Twenty minutes later they set out. Imea and two other men, barefoot, carried the heavy packs, bush knives strapped to the sides. In their hands, they held long black palm spears with wickedly carved bamboo points. Blake and the others carried smaller daypacks.

The entire village had turned out to watch their departure. Men, women and children lined the narrow muddy corridor between the huts as the group walked slowly through the settlement. In front of one of the huts, a dog began to growl. One of the men leaned forward and struck it heavily with the flat of his bush knife, its yelps of pain echoing off the jungle wall in front of them.

Just before they entered the trees at the edge of the clearing, Blake shot a last glance at the ridge in front of them. The clouds were closer now, and darker.

* * *

The narrow trail snaked through the forest, running parallel to the river somewhere off to the right. Thick leaves and vines blocked the sun, creating a shadowy labyrinth through which it was impossible to see for more than five or six feet. Insects and brilliantly colored butterflies darted back and forth across the path, and from their hiding places deeper in the jungle came the shrill cries of birds.

The small party padded in single file through the twilit undergrowth, sweat dripping from their faces and staining their clothes. The air grew ever more humid with every passing moment, as the clouds above the narrow valley descended, pressing on the top of the forest canopy which reared high above the trail. Within the first half hour, Blake's legs had found their stride, and his boots felt comfortable. Ed Jeffries and Jill Winters also walked easily, with no apparent effort. Only Ray Corley showed signs of discomfort as he lurched clumsily along, his breathing audible above the forest noises.

Ahead of them, the guides moved rapidly. Bent over the big packs, they walked with short jerky steps, hopping effortlessly over tree trunks and fallen branches. As they went, they cut large blazes into the trees every few yards with their bush knives. They can walk us into the ground, Blake thought with wry amusement. Damn good thing they're carrying most of the weight.

From far away in the jungle came a deep boom, followed by a momentary silence from the birds and insects. Everyone stopped.

"What was that?" asked Winters.

Imea smiled. "Big tree falling. Moss on the trees collects rainwater, becomes very heavy. The old trees fall down." He looked around. "We don't like to be in the forest after the rain. Many things here are dangerous."

Winters looked at him. "What else is dangerous?"

Imea's smile disappeared. "Snakes," he said. "And people."

He did not elaborate. He turned and kept walking.

* * *

Blake called a halt after the first hour.

"What are we stopping for?" demanded Jeffries, striding up the trail. "We're still fresh. We should keep going."

Blake shook his head. "We need to eat and drink something now, and tighten our bootlaces. A rest every hour or so will keep our energy levels up. We'll get going again in a couple of minutes. Too long, and our muscles will cramp."

The guides set their loads down some distance away, talking softly among themselves and watching the group warily. Blake unpacked chocolate and raisins and distributed them, walking up the trail to hand some to the guides.

When he returned, Winters had pulled her boots off and was staring at her foot in horror. "God," she gasped. "They're disgusting!"

Blake saw three fat leeches dug into her bare ankle, each one the size of a cigar butt.

"Hold still." He took a cigarette from one of the spare packets and shredded it, rubbing the raw tobacco over the blood-gorged leeches. A moment later their bloated bodies began to convulse, and a few seconds later, they dropped to the ground. Blood continued to flow freely from the wounds on her ankle.

"Don't worry about the bleeding," Blake told her. "They use an anti-coagulant to keep it going. It'll stop soon." He turned to the others. "Better check your boots, gentlemen."

Both men also found leeches on their legs, and removed them with tobacco the way Blake had shown them.

"They're ugly, but fairly harmless," Blake explained. "You can get rid of them with almost anything irritating – salt, kerosene, tobacco."

The guides had drawn near during this time, and now they carefully collected the leeches and began to pull them to bits, grinding them to paste on a flat rock with their bush knives. One of them grinned at Blake and pointed at the ground. Blake glanced down and saw half a dozen more leeches hunching across the rotting leaves towards his boots, attracted by the smell of blood.

"Time to get moving," he said, shouldering his pack.

Winters fell into step beside him. "Thanks, Peter," she said with a grin. "They never taught us that one in my nursing course."

He smiled back at her. "We'll see some more of those today, but they'll disappear as we move higher. They keep strictly to the rainforest."

She pushed back her damp hair and looked up at the trail ahead. "How long before we come to the start of the ridge?"

"A few more miles, I think. Then things will get more difficult." He glanced back at Corley. The man was gulping water from his canteen, his face flushed and tense. There's our weak link for sure, Blake thought. He's the one who'll break first. We'll have to watch him all the time.

He felt Winters' hand on his arm. "You're worried about him, aren't you?" She kept her voice low.

"Yes," he said. "We can only move as fast as the slowest member. We'll have to help each other, and him especially."

From up ahead, Jeffries' voice rang out. "Come on, pick up the pace! We haven't got all day!"

Winters looked back again at Corley, a worried frown on her lips.

# CHAPTER SIX

The rain began at noon. Gentle at first, it soon became a steady downpour. The forest sounds gradually disappeared under the roar of falling water, as the world was transformed into a sodden ruin. Water was suddenly everywhere. It dripped from the leaves and vines; it ran underfoot in small rivulets. It nested in shallow pools on the ground and in depressions in the fallen trees that littered the forest floor. In a matter of minutes, the forest became a swamp.

The first accident happened an hour later.

They had come around a bend in the trail to find a stream, swollen suddenly with rainwater, blocking their way. Now they huddled close together on the high bank, staring silently at the turmoil below, as tons of rushing water boiled down through the rocky channel. Beyond the stream, the trail continued steeply upward. There it is, thought Blake; the beginning of the ridge leading to the plateau. But first we have to get across this.

Two enormous logs straddled the torrent, their sides dark with moss and glistening with rain. One of the guides had taken off his pack and was walking out along the logs, testing them, calling back to Imea who stood on the bank beside Blake, a worried look on his face.

"The log on the right is good," Imea yelled over the noise of the rain and current. "The other is rotten. Don't step on it!"

Blake planted one of his boots experimentally on the good log. It slid off as though greased. Taking one of the heavy climbing ropes from his pack, he uncoiled it and gave one end to Imea. "Tie this around yourself and walk across. When you get there, tie it to a tree."

The man nodded and stepped out carefully onto the log.

In five minutes Imea was safe on the other side and had attached the rope. Blake tied a length of parachute cord around a tree, clipped a carabiner to the cord, and snapped the climbing rope into the carabiner. He handed the end of the rope to Winters and Corley.

"Pull this taut," Blake said. "Now you've got a handrail, see?"

Blake took off his boots, tied the laces together, and slung them around his neck. "I'm going across," he said. "I think this might work better if we're barefoot." He picked up the second coil of climbing rope and clipped the end to his waist.

He turned to Winters. "Grab the other end of this and hold on to it. When I get there, I'll set up a belay. Then we'll get everyone else across, one by one. The guides go first. Then you, Jill. Then Jeffries. You tie the rope around your waist, and I'll have you on the other end. Take your boots off, you'll get a better grip that way, and keep hold of the guide rope. When each one crosses, I'll throw the rope back across the stream for the next person."

He turned to Corley. "Ray, you'll come last. Now keep that guide rope taut, you two."

The guides crossed quickly and without difficulty, balancing their heavy loads delicately, staring at the rushing water below. Then Winters came across, more hesitantly, more awkwardly.

As she stepped off the log and onto the bank beside Blake, he said, "Grab the other end of the handrail rope and pull it tight – it's starting to sag. Ray, you tighten it up on your end. Make it nice and taut."

From the opposite bank, Corley nodded.

Blake looped the second rope around his waist, sat down on the bank, and braced his feet firmly against some large tree roots. He took up the rope's slack and settled into position. "Okay, Ed," he yelled across the torrent. "Start walking!"

Jeffries stepped out on the log and glanced down at the water, hissing through the rocky channel ten feet below.

"Don't lean on the guide rope, man!" Blake shouted. "Just hold it for balance. And don't step on the other log. Now come on."

With tiny hesitant steps, Jeffries edged slowly out along the log until he had come nearly halfway. Then he froze. His eyes rose to meet Blake's. "The goddamn log is slippery as hell," he said in a tight voice, barely audible above the water. "I can't—"

"Keep going," said Blake. "I've got you – everything's okay. And hurry up, for God's sake." To the others he said, "Keep that guide rope taut."

Just then the guide rope seemed to dip. Jeffries, clutching it with one hand, was thrown off balance. Panic-stricken, he did an awkward little shuffle. His weight shifted, and his foot came down solidly on the rotten log. Behind Blake, Winters drew her breath in sharply.

With a dull crack, the log broke in two. With a shout, Jeffries fell straight down, into the rapids below. The swift current pulled him under immediately.

Blake cursed as the belay rope whipped tight, burning his hands. He strained at the rope, gripping it desperately, hauling with all his might. Seconds later, Jeffries' head broke water, his body turning over and over in the rushing current.

"Look!"

Winters' shout made Blake raise his eyes to where the broken log hung a few feet above the water, its splintered ends dipping closer to the furious current. In a matter of seconds, he realized, the water would catch the jagged ends and whirl them down directly on top of Jeffries.

Straining, he played the big man like a fish, edging him closer to the bank downstream, away from danger. Imea had already scrambled down the muddy slope and now stood ready, his arms reaching out.

Blake let the rope out a bit more and finally maneuvered Jeffries into a relatively quiet pool of water. Imea jumped in and grabbed him by the shirt, dragging him to the safety of the bank. A moment later, the broken log fell with a crash into the current, flashing swiftly past the point where Jeffries had been floating a minute earlier.

Blake dropped the rope and plunged down through the bushes to where Jeffries lay gasping for air, his boots still miraculously around his neck. He coughed, spitting up water, and got unsteadily to his feet.

"Are you all right?" Blake asked.

Jeffries looked at him, the panic in his eyes subsiding. "I think so," he said finally. He glanced up the bank. "No thanks to those two, though."

"What are you talking about?"

"The guide rope," Jeffries said, in a low, angry voice. "One of them moved the fucking guide rope. That's why I lost my balance. Didn't you see it, for God's sake?"

Blake shook his head. "I wasn't watching them, I was watching you," he said shortly. "Anyway, you're imagining things. Come on, let's get back to the others."

Jeffries grabbed Blake's arm. "I didn't imagine a damned thing. That bloody rope moved."

Blake shook himself free. "We've got enough problems, Jeffries, without you looking for trouble over this. You'd have been all right if you'd kept your weight off the rope. Just be glad you're alive. Come on."

As Blake watched Jeffries clamber up the slippery bank, he thought about what he had said. Jeffries was right; the guide rope had gone slack. Just before he fell.

He shook his head. But it couldn't have been deliberate, could it? No, that was silly; it didn't make any sense. He sighed. We've been lucky so far, he thought. But there'll be more accidents before the trip's over. And how long will our luck hold?

* * *

Stripped to shorts and T-shirts now, they inched their way steadily up the ridge, the trail growing ever steeper. Blake stood at the side of the muddy track, looking at his altimeter and frowning.

Jeffries staggered up, stopped, and wiped his forehead. "What's the problem, Blake?"

"We're going too slowly," Blake said. "In the last thirty minutes we've only come up about three hundred feet." He looked up at the crack of sky showing through the forest canopy. "It'll be dark at six o'clock. We've got to find water and a place to camp before that."

Jeffries slapped at a stinging fly on his shoulder and grimaced. "I can make it, Blake. Save your breath for that guy there." He jerked his thumb back along the trail to where Ray Corley sat on a rotted log, gasping for breath and wiping water from his face with a filthy handkerchief.

In the gloom of the drowned forest, his face looked pinched and pale, gleaming like a plump death's head in the dim light. From somewhere far inside the forest, a bird screamed. Overhead, the rain continued to fall.

Jill Winters materialized from around the trail's bend and slumped down next to Corley, breathing hard. Her soaked hair plastered her face, and her tanned arms and legs showed dozens of tiny bites and scratches.

They've all become increasingly unmindful of the insects and leeches, Blake thought as he walked back to her. Too tired to care much anymore.

She looked up at him, and then at Corley. "He's exhausted," she said. "And I'm not far behind him. My God, this is a dreadful place." She paused to wipe water from her face with hands that were pale and wrinkled from the humidity. "Ugh."

"I've got some glucose tablets in my pack," said Blake. "Both of you should take some. They'll help for a while, anyway."

She stood up and brushed hair out of her eyes. "How much longer are we going to keep on with this, Peter? I don't think I can take much more."

He checked his watch. "We've got to gain more altitude. We've only climbed a few thousand feet since we left the village. If we're going to reach the plateau tomorrow, we've got to get higher."

Jeffries squatted down beside them. "I agree with Blake," he said. "The more we do today, the less we do tomorrow."

Winters shuddered. "Easier said than done," she muttered, handing Corley the tube of glucose tablets. "It will only make things worse if we push too hard, you know."

Blake knew all too well. The more exhausted they got, the greater the risk of another accident. It would be a simple matter, for example, to slip on the muddy trail and break an ankle. He'd seen it happen before. The slightest moment of inattention could lead to disaster. Even death. He shivered, thinking again of Becky, high on the cliff face.

He stood up and shrugged on his rucksack. "Three hours to sundown," he said. "Three hours to find somewhere dry and safe. Let's get moving."

"I understand the part about dry," muttered Winters as they began to trudge up the trail again. "But safe? I thought there weren't any really dangerous animals in New Guinea. Except for the snakes, of course."

"There aren't," Blake replied. "But that's not what I had in mind. According to my estimates, we crossed the border about an hour ago. Right now we're in Indonesia – on enemy territory, so to speak."

# CHAPTER SEVEN

Ray Corley crouched under the eaves of the hunter's shelter in the gathering darkness and fumbled with the stove. Fuel dribbled from the aluminum bottle soaking the ground near his still-burning cigarette.

Blake moved swiftly, grinding out the man's cigarette and taking the bottle from him. "Be careful with that stuff," he cautioned. "Stove fuel's volatile as hell – it'll go up like a bomb." He pointed to the pandanus-leafed interior of the shelter. "Go on inside and lie down for a few minutes. I'll get the stove going."

Corley nodded gratefully and shuffled off. Blake lit the stove and put water on to boil. Then he uncorked the whiskey bottle and poured everyone a stiff drink.

"Drink up," he said, handing the cups round. "Help me lighten tomorrow's load."

As they sipped their whiskey, Blake noticed the color beginning to return to Corley's face. Good, Blake thought, he won't die just yet. Not today at any rate.

Sitting down on his sleeping bag, he stared out at the jungle. Right before dark, they'd found a relatively level spot just off the trail. Ten minutes' work with bush knives had cleared enough space for them to set up a makeshift camp. There wasn't likely to be any more rain tonight, so Blake had suggested that they sleep outside their tents. Later on, at the higher altitudes, they'd be grateful for the warmth of the tents, but here, being in the open air was welcome. Imea and the guides had quickly constructed several open lean-tos instead, using branches, broad leaves and vines.

Near the edge of the clearing, the guides talked quietly as they boiled rice over a small wood fire in front of their shelter. The rain had stopped an hour ago, the forest quiet now as it slowly subsided into night, with only an occasional drip of water to intrude on the silence. The air had turned cooler; the mist left behind by the rain had settled down into the valley bottoms below. Overhead, Blake caught a glimpse of bright stars through the trees.

"How high do you think we are now?" Winters' voice broke the spell.

Blake grimaced. "Not high enough. Altimeter says just over eight thousand feet. We've got another two thousand to go before we reach the plateau. And the trail will get tougher tomorrow."

At this, Corley groaned.

"Shut up," growled Jeffries. "If it weren't for you, we'd be a lot further along. You're the slowest of the group – the one that's holding us back."

"Leave him alone," snapped Winters. "You were the one who fell off the log into the river, remember? That wasted a good half an hour."

Jeffries opened his mouth to reply, but Blake cut him off. "Stop," he said. "Both of you. We're all here, safe and dry, and that's a victory, believe me." He poured more whiskey for each of them. "Finish this while I get dinner."

He got up and moved to his pack. Selecting dried meat, soup powder and freeze-dried vegetables, he threw everything together into a pot of water and set it on the hissing stove. He looked up to see Corley pulling radio equipment from his pack and assembling it.

"What's he doing over there?" he asked Winters.

"He's setting up to take a bearing on the nose cone," she replied. "We're high enough now to catch the signal. If we can get a couple of different readings, we can pinpoint its location."

The stew began to simmer. Blake turned it down and walked over to where Ray Corley crouched, bent over his instruments. "Find anything?"

Corley took off his headphones and reached for the map. "The signal's weak, but it's there, all right." With his pencil, he drew a line intersecting the mountain crest, just below Antares's summit. "Right where it ought to be." He grinned. "Worked almost perfectly."

From out of the darkness across the clearing came Jeffries' voice. "Our Ray Corley is a man of many talents. He not only built the satellite, he figured out how to drive it, too."

"Jill and I built it, actually," Corley said. "SkyScan was our project. We spent years developing it, working nights, weekends, you name it. I built him the best damned piece of satellite technology in existence. And Jill designed the data collection system, everything from scratch." He turned to look at Blake, his eyes hard. "We gave the sonofabitch years of our lives, and you know what happened? Once he had his precious satellite and its data system, he got rid of us."

"You mean he fired you?"

"Terminated all of us. The whole unit. Once he had what he wanted, he didn't need us anymore. He held up our non-disclosure agreements as he did it, told us he'd bury us in lawsuits if we went to work for anyone else." Corley's expression darkened. "Well, fuck that. What goes up can also come down. I took the codes, everything, with me."

He looked at Blake. "I never trusted the guy, not really. I always thought he might pull something like this. So I made sure I had backdoor systems designed into the thing that only I could control, just in case I had to. At first, I thought I'd just send a virus in and wreck the thing. But then" – he glanced over at Jeffries – "I met Amos Sanford, and he gave me a better idea."

Corley's glasses glinted in the firelight. "You have any idea how hard it is to bring one of these things down in a precise spot? No, of course you don't. But I do. I can." He grinned triumphantly. "And I bloody well did."

Jeffries spoke again from the darkness. "You're not as good as you think you are, Ray. Otherwise we wouldn't be up here in the fucking jungle looking for the thing."

"Go to hell, Ed. If it weren't for me, we wouldn't have anything to actually look for." He began to pack his gear away. "We're going to need at least one more bearing to determine the nose cone's precise position. How far are we from this plateau you were talking about earlier?"

Blake shrugged. "Couple of miles, more or less."

"That should give us enough of an angle. I'll take another reading once we get there." He grimaced. "If the nose cone's batteries last that long, that is."

Jeffries cleared his throat. "So we'll have to make it to the plateau tomorrow, won't we?" He looked at Corley, who had picked up his tin cup of whiskey again. "That means no more sauce tonight, Ray. Understand?"

"Screw you, Ed. I'll do my job here, don't you worry." Corley's voice had gone high and reedy. He took off his thick glasses and began to polish them with trembling hands. In the hissing light of the gas lantern, his eyes looked tired and puffy.

Blake stood up. "We could all move a little faster, you know, if we didn't have all this extra gear. I understand what Corley's signal finder does, but what are these things for?" He pointed to two small grey metal boxes with knobs, buttons and dials.

"That's my equipment," said Winters. She pointed to the larger of the boxes. "This is a transceiver. We can receive and transmit up to about two hundred miles. Somewhat more at night."

"Could you raise Hagen Tower with it?"

"If we had to, yes. That's why I brought it. Amos has got a receiver; I'll call him when we come down off the mountain, so he'll know to come pick us up," said Winters.

"And the other box?"

"Amos suggested that. It's a beacon; it broadcasts a navigational beam on a fixed frequency."

Blake frowned. "What good is that?"

"It's for emergency use, as a sort of homing device. If we had to radio for help – for a helicopter, for instance – we'd use the transceiver. But the beacon would actually be able to guide the chopper to our exact location, in just the same way that we're zeroing in on the nose cone. We can also use the beacon in case we split up. One party takes the transceiver, the other takes the beacon. That way, one group can always find the other."

Blake nodded. "Impressive."

Winters smiled. "Not really. You can buy this stuff in almost any electronics store. The impressive thing is this." She reached under her T-shirt and pulled out what looked like a flash drive, attached to a lanyard.

"And what is that?"

"That," said Winters with a wink, "is top secret." Catching Blake's expression, she grinned. "At least, that's what Boomer Barrett thinks. You see, the satellite's data isn't transmitted down to earth, it's stored in the nose cone. So that nobody else can intercept the signal. That's why we have to find the nose cone; the data's all stored inside it, in a module. And that data is encrypted. Even if you downloaded it, it wouldn't make any sense."

She held up the flash drive. "Unless you had this, too. It decrypts whatever the satellite's collected." She smiled again. "That is, it will if somebody inputs the right codes. And there's only one person who knows those codes – me."

"So you got fired, along with Ray?" asked Blake.

Winters nodded. "World's biggest bastard. My story is a little different from Ray's, but neither of us owe that asshole a thing."

"And now you both work for Amos Sanford."

Her eyes flashed. "I don't work for anyone, Peter. This is me and me alone. I just want to mess up Barrett's operation, and if I can make some money in the process, so much the better."

Jeffries walked over to stand beside them. "Private enterprise in operation, Blake. Amos reached out to Corley, and once they'd connected, Corley brought Jill in. It wasn't hard. Amos is always looking out ahead of things. Like what that hockey player said one time, you want to think where the puck is going to be, and go there... Once we get our hands on that data, Amos can sell it for a fortune."

Blake began dishing out the meal he'd prepared. "I guess I'm impressed," he said as he passed their plates around. "But remember what I said: the mountain makes its own rules. All the fancy equipment in the world won't help us if we break those rules."

He looked around the group. "We'll be okay, as long as we're very, very careful." His gaze rested for a moment on Ed Jeffries. "And as long as we look out for each other. Now let's eat and then get some sleep. We've got a very long day tomorrow."

* * *

Blake lay in his sleeping bag, listening to the soft whine of insects around him, and thinking. It was make or break tomorrow, one way or the other. If they couldn't get to the *kunai* before the satellite's signals ceased, they'd be looking for a needle in a haystack at thirteen thousand feet. So, tomorrow, they had to push hard.

But pushing too hard would be dangerous. That would drain their last reserves of energy too soon, and in straining their bodies beyond safe limits, they would give themselves no chance to adjust to the drastic changes in temperature and altitude that awaited them.

Which might lead to more accidents. Serious ones.

Blake fell asleep thinking of the high country which lay ahead, his body sweating in the sleeping bag in the quiet jungle clearing.

# CHAPTER EIGHT

If there's a hell on earth, Blake thought wearily, then this is surely it. Soaked to the skin and sore in every part of his body, he now had a headache that wouldn't go away. His legs and arms bore innumerable shallow cuts and scrapes where he had brushed against branches and thorns, and his shins itched unbearably from the stings of nettles. His small pack seemed to weigh a thousand pounds, and he was filthy and stinking. Looking up, he saw that the rain was almost upon them again.

They had been climbing since dawn through the damp forest, never able to see more than ten feet in any direction, pursued by relentless clouds of mosquitoes and biting flies. Three o'clock now, and the ridge was becoming shrouded again in a fine cloud of mist, a precursor to the thick clouds creeping down from the peaks above.

The group toiled along slowly, strung out along the steep trail, moving through an eerie landscape of half-seen forms – the mist making strange shapes which writhed slowly in the currents left by their passing. The forest seemed quieter than yesterday, dominated mainly by the group's hoarse breathing and an occasional bird cry from somewhere inside the jungle.

Bad for me, worse for the others, thought Blake grimly. Especially for Ray Corley. Since morning, Corley had moved as if in a sleepwalker's trance. Desperately overtaxed, he lurched along with the drunkard's disregard for balance. They had fed him glucose and water, and taken breaks at increasingly frequent intervals, but it wasn't working anymore. In the meantime, Blake knew that the others were also nearing the end of their reserves.

Far ahead, the guides moved steadily along, hacking a path through the vines and bamboo. Their cuts left rows of razor-sharp sticks at eye level, looking exactly like the deadly points of giant hypodermic needles.

Blake rounded a corner to find himself on the edge of an open clearing of burnt-off stumps and short grass. The mist had yet to reach this spot; overhead, the sun shone brightly. The guides lay sprawled on the ground, smoking and talking, their blankets pulled tight around them to ward off the chill which had crept up in the last hour. Their conversation stopped as soon as they caught sight of Blake.

He shrugged off his pack and checked his altimeter. Nine thousand feet. At their present rate of climb, they would need at least another two hours to reach the *kunai* plateau. He looked at his watch. Barely enough time to get there and make camp before sundown.

Despite the sunshine, the air was noticeably colder now. Blake pulled on his windbreaker as the sweat on his body dried, making him shiver. Ahead, higher on the ridge, the clouds were thick and dropping lower by the second. With them would come more cold rain.

He glanced back down the trail and saw that for the first time in nearly two days, there was actually a view. The clearing lay on a knobby outcropping, providing an excellent open vista of the entire valley back to the east, up through which they had trudged the previous day. The ridge dropped away sharply in front of him, heavily forested and smoky with mist, with only tiny furrows in the dark-green canopy of trees to mark where the streams and rivers ran.

Far in the distance below lay the Wambip airstrip, still bathed in sunlight. It seemed suspended magically in space, wreathed in the faint haze of cooking fires and shimmering slightly in the afternoon light. Ten miles away and more than four thousand feet below, it might as well be on the other side of the earth itself, Blake thought. They had been there only yesterday, but yesterday seemed already centuries ago. Today, there was no reality other than the forest and the steep muddy trail.

Imea, a cigarette dangling from his mouth, came to squat beside Blake. "It's not good to stay here too long," he said quietly. "The Indonesians sometimes have soldiers in this area." He pointed to a side trail. "There is a patrol post this way."

"Do you see soldiers often?"

Imea shrugged. "We don't come here often. Once in a while, to hunt. If the soldiers see us, they shoot at us."

The two men were silent for a moment. "The other men are afraid," Imea said. "The mountain is a bad place, and they are afraid." He gazed steadily at the village below as he spoke.

"Afraid of what?"

Imea threw his cigarette away and turned to face him. "Our people don't like this place. Some of them died here once. Tonight you will sleep on the *kunai* – on the flat grass place. And we will go back to the village, away from here."

"People died here? How did they die?"

Imea pointed to the descending clouds. "The white smoke killed them. First it made them cold. Then it killed them." He shivered, drawing his blanket tight around his thin body. "This place is what we call the mountain's doorway – the place where you enter his house, where you begin to feel his power. The mountain doesn't like people in his house... This place is *tumbuna*. You understand *tumbuna*?"

Blake nodded. "Something old. Something from the time before."

"Yes. From before the white man came. White men have power; they can do many things. But *tumbuna* things are much stronger." He paused. "At mission school where I learned English, they said that Jesus Christ was stronger than *tumbuna*. But our people never saw Jesus Christ kill anybody the way this mountain did."

Imea looked back at his companions and dropped his voice to a whisper. "Before, our people had names for this mountain, the one you call Antares. It was called" – his voice dropped – "Anjila. But then the white man came and gave it a different name, a name for the stars… That is good – the Star Mountains is a good name. That way, the *tumbuna* doesn't hear his real name."

"The old name, Anjila, what does it mean?"

Imea rose to his feet. His face was carefully without expression as he looked at Blake with flat eyes. "It means 'the place where people die'," he whispered. "Don't say the name again." Then he turned away, back to where his companions sat, huddled against the growing chill.

Jill Winters appeared, staggering out of the forest, her face streaked with mud. "Ed and Ray are just behind me," she said as she limped across to sit beside Blake. "My blisters have got blisters. How much more of this do we have to do, for God's sake?"

"Two more hours," replied Blake. "We're nearly there. We'll eat something once the others get here, and take a short rest. But we've got to keep moving if we want to be on the plateau before dark."

"I certainly don't want to have to sleep in this fucking jungle again, not if I can help it. This whole place gives me the creeps." Winters shivered, drawing her parka around her.

"It's Ray, you know," she said in a quiet voice. "He keeps slowing us down, needing to rest. If it weren't for that, we'd be there by now."

Blake agreed. "He's not in the best of physical shape. And it doesn't help that he's a drunk."

Winters squinted at him. "He wasn't always like this, you know. Ray and I worked together for five years. He's a pretty good guy, really. His drinking only got bad after he got fired."

She shook her head. "He was one of the best satellite engineers in the country. What Boomer Barrett did to him really messed up is self-esteem. The worst part was, he couldn't get another job. Oh, he could always open a computer repair shop or something, but nothing like what he'd been doing with Barrett." She looked at Blake. "Boomer destroyed him, Peter. He's got very little left. Now all he wants to do is get even."

"Like you?"

"My reasons are different," she said. "Maybe someday I'll tell you. But not now."

"Then let me ask you another question," said Blake. "I get why there might be a self-destruct mechanism built into the nose cone. But this data module that's inside – the one you need to decrypt in order to use – why do you have to be up here with us at all? Why not let Ray bring you the module down in Port Moresby, or Brisbane, or somewhere else, instead of up here in the middle of the mountains?"

She gave him a tight smile. "Because I don't trust any of them, Peter. I never trusted Boomer Barrett, and I was right to do so. When Ray introduced me to Amos, I decided I didn't really trust him either. So I made sure that whatever the deal was that was going to get made, I had to be a part of it. All the way along, right to the end."

Blake shook his head. "I understand how you feel, but it's going to get a lot tougher in the next day or so. You're going to need to trust someone, whether you like it or not."

She fixed him with her eyes. "I know that, Peter. And I've decided that I trust you."

They fell silent then, each thinking private thoughts. Blake closed his eyes and savored the weak warmth of the sunshine. A shout from one of the guides snapped his eyes open, and a second later, he heard it: a low-pitched whickering noise that seemed to come from everywhere at once. He scrambled to his feet as the noise grew louder, filling the clearing.

"Take cover!" he yelled. "Get under the trees, quick!"

Everyone scrambled for hiding places as the reconnaissance helicopter swung up and around the side of the ridge, headed straight toward them.

Blake recognized it as a Huey, and as it approached, he could make out the military roundel, painted over the camouflage stripes, together with the words 'ANGKATAN DARAT'. He whipped out his binoculars and focused. There were only two men inside; the pilot and a spotter, holding binoculars as he swept the forest below.

Blake dropped his own binoculars and pushed Winters down into the leaves. "Don't move," he hissed. "They're coming right overhead."

The world was filled with noise as the chopper thundered by overhead, barely fifty feet above the clearing. Then it was gone, up over the side of the ridge to the south. The noise of the rotors dropped off sharply. Blake waited a moment until he was sure they weren't coming back. Then he crawled out from under the bushes and brushed himself off.

Jeffries burst from the forest. "What the hell was that?" he said, gasping for breath.

"Indonesian border patrol," Blake answered. "A helicopter, headed south. Probably on a run from Jayapura down to Merauke."

"Christ! Did they spot you?"

"Don't think so. We heard them just in time."

"Jesus." Jeffries stood there for a moment, a worried frown on his face. "We'd better get going, then. Before they decide to come back." He turned and started up the trail.

Blake put a hand on his shoulder. "Wait." He pointed down the valley. "Look – down there. Something's going on."

They all saw it this time – a flash of light, moving slowly; reflections from the wings of an aircraft, making its way up the valley toward the landing strip at Wambip.

Blake raised his binoculars again, adjusting the focus, just as a faint drone of motors reached his ears. "It's an Islander," he said after a moment. "Like the one we came in. And it's landing in the village." As he watched, the plane touched down at the end of the grass runway, props flashing in the late afternoon sunlight as the pilot reversed pitch.

"There aren't supposed to be any flights today," Jeffries murmured.

"That's right," said Blake, keeping the glasses trained on the plane. "Wait – someone's getting out. No – two people. Two men. They've got bags – no, backpacks, it looks like."

Jeffries snatched the glasses. "Let me see."

From the valley below came the faint sound of motors being revved. The plane, impossibly small in the distance, wheeled and started back down the airstrip, accelerating rapidly.

"They're staying behind," said Jeffries, "those two men." He stood up and handed the glasses back to Blake. "That's it, then. I should have known. We'd better get going, fast."

"Hold on a minute," said Blake. "Who are those men? What's all this about?"

Jeffries shook his head. "I'll explain later. No time now. Come on, everybody back on the trail!"

Blake looked around. "Where's Ray?" he said to Jeffries. "I thought he was with you."

"Yes," said Winters, getting to her feet. "Where is Ray?"

* * *

They found Ray Corley ten minutes later, lying along the side of the trail, his back against a tree. He might have been sleeping, but when Blake reached over to shake him, he spotted the bright blood oozing through his trouser leg.

Dropping to her knees in the mud, Jill Winters rolled up Corley's trouser leg to reveal an ugly three-inch gash just below the knee, wide and still bleeding. Several leeches clung to the edges of the wound. Opening his shirt, she put her ear to his chest, listening for a heartbeat.

"He seems okay," she said a moment later. "Get me the first aid kit from my pack. Quickly."

While she cleaned and dressed the wound, Ed Jeffries fumed. "Dumb sonofabitch," he muttered. "Can't even walk a straight line without falling down. We oughta—"

"Shut up." Blake's eyes blazed. "This is your fault." He grabbed Jeffries by the shirt and pulled him upright. "Don't you know how dangerous it is to leave someone alone in the forest? Even for a few minutes? Goddamnit, I told you this morning to keep him in sight!"

Jeffries broke free. "What the hell am I supposed to be, Blake, his goddamn nursemaid? Everybody's got to pull their own weight here. It's not my fault if he can't take it!" He swung wildly at Blake, missed, and fell with a roar into the mud.

The guides watched silently, not moving a muscle, their hands on their bush knives.

Blake stood over Jeffries, grabbed him by the shirt and hauled him upright. "Listen to me," he hissed. "We either all get up the mountain, or none of us do. We have to do this together. We can't afford emergencies now – not even small ones. We're stretched as thin as possible."

Blake let go of him and backed off, watching the big man carefully. Jeffries glared back, his hands clenched in anger.

"If you two have finished," Winters said, "I think Ray's coming to. Ed, get me some water for him."

Jeffries looked at her for a moment, shrugged, and bent to his pack.

When Corley had managed a few sips, Blake squatted down beside him. "Now," he said, "tell us what happened."

Corley shook his head to clear it. "I– I fell down. Hard. Just there." He indicated a broken log across the path. "And when I got up again, there was blood pouring down my leg."

He looked up, a forlorn expression on his face.

"I guess I passed out," he said, blinking behind his thick glasses. "It's the blood, you see. I can't stand looking at blood. Even when I was a kid–" He stopped suddenly, bent his head, and vomited.

When his spasms had stopped, Blake pulled him gently to his feet. "Try to walk," he said.

Corley took a few experimental steps and stopped, pain twisting his face. "Jesus," he breathed, tightening his grip on Blake's shoulder. "That hurts."

They sat him down again. Winters took off his boot and inspected his ankle. "Not broken," she said after a moment. "But probably badly twisted. He really shouldn't put any weight on it right now."

Blake looked up at the sky. The clouds were directly overhead now, and even as he stared at them, he heard the whisper of the first raindrops striking the forest canopy. "That's it," he said heavily. "We'll camp here tonight. If he's not better tomorrow, we go back." His eyes met Winters'. "There's nothing else we can do. He can't go on."

"No, Blake." Jeffries' voice was dangerously low. "We're going on. We're going to get to the plateau tonight." He indicated the guides. "They can rig a hammock and carry him if they have to."

Blake opened his mouth to protest. He closed it again at the sight of the small but deadly-looking automatic pistol which Jeffries held in his hand. Its muzzle was pointed straight at his belt.

"No more discussion, Blake." Jeffries spoke in a hoarse voice. "You do what I say from now on." Sweat gleamed on his face. The forest was quiet, except for the harsh sound of his breathing and the gentle patter of the rain.

# CHAPTER NINE

The two tents crouched at the far end of the *kunai* plateau, up against the eaves of the forest. A mile away across the short grassy plain, the rock wall reared up, black and featureless in the night, blotting out the stars.

Blake sat under the tent fly, a hot dinner in his belly and a cup of the last of the whiskey in his hand, drying out after the day's rain. He watched the sputtering campfire, feelings his aches and pains slowly receding. They all needed rest badly, he thought. All of them were over-extended. Dangerously so. Tomorrow they would rest, and he would study the cliff with his binoculars, searching for a route to the top.

And the day after that, they would climb it.

Jeffries had let loose with a whoop of triumph when they had finally staggered out onto the plateau in the late afternoon. Blake didn't bother to tell him that getting to the top of the ridge was but a small victory. The real challenges still lay in front of them. The guides, plainly uncomfortable, had left them at the edge of the plateau and turned back into the forest, heading back to the village.

It's been a feat of sorts to get even this far, Blake reflected as he sipped his whiskey, but now there's the cliff to climb. Two thousand feet high, it presented a formidable and dangerous obstacle to an untrained team.

And beyond that lay the summit ridge itself, and perhaps further obstacles.

And untrained they certainly are, Blake thought. They had used up most of their luck getting up the ridge. A day of rest would restore some of their energy, but you couldn't recoup luck or reverse the odds.

Winters came and sat beside him. "What are you thinking about? Warm afternoons on the reef, I'll bet."

"No." Blake shook his head, pointing to the dark mass of the cliff. "That."

She shivered. "It's freezing up here," she said as she zipped her parka tighter. "Will it be much colder on top?"

Blake nodded. "Below freezing at night. Frost in the mornings. Maybe some snow."

She stared at him. "Snow? On the equator? Seriously?"

"The Stars are often snow-capped. Further to the west, Carstensz has an actual glacier. There's also the wind," he added. "It doesn't take much of a breeze to bring the wind chill factor down to around zero."

Winters thought about all of that for a moment. "How difficult is this really going to be, Peter? To get up there, I mean?"

He shrugged. "I'll need to see the cliff properly first," he said. "We'll take a look tomorrow with the binoculars, and figure out a route up."

Winters was silent, staring into the blackness beyond the campfire. "Funny how quiet it is," she said finally. "There's no noise at all, is there? I read somewhere that in inhabited places, there's always a sort of background hum from machinery or electricity or something. But here – we're really alone, aren't we? I've never been in a place like this before – so far away from everything. And we're on our own now, without the guides."

She turned to him. "You enjoy it, don't you? Being on your own up here. I can tell you do. I can tell from the way you move. You seem much more – well, more alive, somehow."

"I've always liked the mountains," he admitted. "In the same way that I like the sea. They're total environments. When you're in them, it's on their terms, not yours. And every decision you take is consequential. Climbing is physically demanding, but it's mentally challenging as well." He looked around. "It's hard to get that sort of feeling – of aliveness – in many other situations."

"But you don't much like being with us, do you? I can tell that, too. We're making you jumpy, aren't we?"

Blake threw a stick on the fire, making it flare up suddenly. "There's bound to be tension," he said carefully after a moment. "We're on borrowed time. We're intruders, Jill, we shouldn't be here at all, not really. Not with people like Ray, and Ed. Sooner or later, something's going to happen. And the longer we stay, the more dangerous it gets." He looked over at her. "No, I don't like being with the group. Not at all."

"Then why are you doing this?" she asked softly. "I know Sanford's got some sort of hold on you, but I don't know what it is. Can you tell me?"

Blake sighed and set his cup down. In short, toneless sentences, he told her of his involvement with the environmental activists. About the sabotage operation that had gone wrong, his flight from the authorities. The months spent moving from place to place across Southeast Asia, until he'd finally landed in Papua New Guinea and begun to build a quiet life for himself again, making a bit of money from his specimen collecting and, on occasion, guiding groups into the high country.

"Doesn't sound that exciting," she said when he had finished.

"I'm not looking for exciting," he said quietly. "I'm looking for safe. Safe and out of sight. In a few more years, the statute of limitations will run out on the stuff I was charged with. Maybe I'll go back then." He sipped his whiskey. "Or maybe I'll just sail around the islands in the Laurabada."

"That's your boat, isn't it? How did you come by a boat?"

Blake gave a dry chuckle. "Stroke of good luck, really. I picked up the Laurabada from a burn-out; a guy who'd started out from San Diego with his wife and another couple. They were going to sail around the world and write a book about it. By the time they put in at Moresby three weeks later, one guy's wife had walked out on him in Papeete and he'd started screwing the other guy's woman. They all had a fight one night down at the Royal Papua Yacht Club, and he got brained with a champagne bottle. Fractured his skull. They had to evacuate him south to Brisbane for surgery. She sold me the boat for the price of a first-class airfare home."

"Wow," breathed Winters. After a moment she said, "Well, I think you made the right choice, Peter, leaving the States like that. I would have done the same, in your place."

"I had a choice between fighting things out in the courts, and running. I'm not sure it was the smart thing to do." He paused, gazing into the fire. "I don't like the running, the hiding. I'm tired of it."

"Did you leave someone behind?"

He was quiet for a moment. "In a way," he said finally. "In grad school I met Becky. I'd always been a rock climber, ever since junior high school back in Utah. Becky was a climber, too. You don't meet too many women who are brilliant, beautiful, and good at free climbing. We started going on weekend trips together, and things just developed from there. We got engaged a year later, while we were on a climbing trip in the Tetons. Two days later, she was dead."

He described the freak storm, the badly set piton, the fall down the sheer face. Everything except the expression in Becky's eyes just before she came off the rock.

"I was responsible for her life, you see," he concluded. "I failed her, and she died... I quit grad school, quit climbing, swore I'd never climb again. I hitchhiked to Portland, met up with some old friends there. I was angry, and I was very much at a loose end. I joined one of the environmental action groups, started doing... stuff, with them. Six months later, our protest operation went sideways, and the law came for me. Since then, I've been too busy running."

"And yet here you are, climbing again," she said. "How do you feel about that?"

He laughed bitterly. "Sanford didn't leave me much of a choice, did he?"

"It must be lonely," she said after a moment. "Being on your own for so long like that."

"You get used to it," he said shortly. "Travel light, travel fast." He looked over at her. "Other people can only slow you down. Like now. Jeffries is right, in a way – if we didn't have Ray Corley with us, we might stand a chance. But the way things are going..." He let the sentence trail off into the night.

"Ray will be all right tomorrow," Winters said. "He's resting comfortably now, and the swelling in his ankle's gone down. I gave him aspirin for his headache, and I'll give him a sleeping pill when we've done the radio for tonight. We need one more bearing to fix the nose cone's position, and nighttime is good for finding weak signals. Ed Jeffries is over there with him now. In a little while I'll go over and help Ray plot the signal."

"There's something I don't understand," said Blake. "Sanford said that you were a data specialist. But you're also a nurse, right? That's an unlikely combination."

"I'm only a nurse because I had to be, Peter. I've got a doctorate in software design from Caltech. Ray got his degrees from Carnegie Mellon. We were a team, for years. My nursing courses came later."

She picked at the zipper of her parka. "I– I used to be married, Peter. Ward – my husband – died last year. He had a rare form of leukemia."

Blake looked at her, not speaking.

She stared into the fire. "Ward was a big, healthy man," she said, her voice low. "But in the end, he wasted away to almost nothing. It took him three years to die. At the end, I could hold him in my arms like a small child." She looked at Blake. "Have you any idea what that's like? He was a lovely, smart, creative man. He was a painter, and we lived mainly on my salary." She swallowed. "I needed to take care of him. I learned nursing so that I could do for him what he needed, once I brought him home."

"I'm sorry," Blake said softly.

She shook her head. "Oh, that's not the half of it, Peter. Not by a long shot. You see, all that time, all the time Ward was sick, Ray and I and the others on the team were working like dogs, finishing the SkyScan programming for Barrett. We worked our hearts out on it, and you know why? Because we believed it would do some good in the world. It was designed to find the kinds of critical minerals – nickel, chromium, cobalt, stuff like that – that we need to develop electric vehicles and solar panels. To reduce our use of fossil fuels. Over time, Ray and I realized that Boomer didn't care a bit about that, not at all – he just wanted the data to sell, to the highest bidder."

She looked up. "And you know who that turned out to be? The fossil fuel industry. They wanted the data, not to use it, but to bury it. And that turned out to be Boomer's plan all along."

Winters gave a low, bitter laugh, and continued. "He waited until the system was all set up, everything ready to go. And then he terminated the entire unit, all in one afternoon. No advance notice, no thank-yous, no nothing. He called us into his office and just fired us, on the spot. Security walked us out, five minutes later."

She wiped her eyes. "And the very best part of all? Our benefits got cancelled the day we were let go. By noon on that day, I had no more health insurance – no way to pay for the drugs, the care, the consultations, for Ward. That's why I took nursing courses – that's why I brought him home. Because I– because I simply couldn't pay the costs anymore.

"I tried, but it was hopeless. He died eventually, of course, and once I lost my job and my insurance, I was very poor indeed." She grimaced. "Later on, I lost the house as well – I had to sell it to pay the medical costs. And so of course it was just about at that time that Amos made contact with me. He'd already talked to Ray. Together they'd come up with this idea, and when he explained it to me, I joined in right away."

"And what is Amos planning to do with the data?" Blake asked softly. "Assuming we recover it, of course."

Winters laughed bitterly. "He'll probably do just what Boomer was going to do. The point is, I personally don't care anymore. Amos isn't a very nice man, Peter, but he's given me and Ray a chance to get back at Boomer Barrett, and hurt him badly. And who knows; we might even make some money out of this when it's all over."

She bit her lip. "So now you know all about it. I'm sorry if I went on too long, Peter. I'll shut up now. I guess I'd really rather not talk any more about it."

Behind them, footsteps approached. Blake turned to see Jeffries coming from Corley's tent, a map in his hand.

"All set," Jeffries said as he stooped to slosh the last of the whiskey into his cup. "We've got an accurate fix on the nose cone now."

Winters looked at him in surprise. "You took the bearing? I thought I was—"

"Relax. You were busy talking to Blake here. The equipment's simple enough, anyway." He unfolded the map and pointed with a thick finger. "Here it is – almost on top of Antares, right up on the bloody crest where we thought it might be." He tossed his drink down. "Now all we have to do is get there." He peered out through the darkness at the outline of the cliff. "How long to climb the wall, Blake?"

"A day, if we find a good route. Tomorrow while the others are resting, I'll check it out."

Jeffries swung around to stare at him. "Nobody's going to be resting, Blake. We're going up that wall, first thing tomorrow morning."

Blake shook his head. "No way. We all need rest, especially Ray. We need—"

"I'll be the judge of what we need, Blake. You're nothing but the trail guide on this trip, remember? We're going up tomorrow morning. Before the clouds move in."

Blake set his cup down. "What are you going to do, Ed? Pull out your gun again? That might impress the locals, but it won't work on me a second time. You need me to get you up the mountain, don't forget that. And we'll do it on my terms, not yours."

Jeffries shook his head. "It's not up to either of us anymore, Blake. Remember that plane we saw landing down in the village earlier today? The two guys who got out? They didn't look like tourists to me."

Blake started to say something, and then closed his mouth.

"And another thing," Jeffries continued, "our guides cut blazes into the trees on the way up. They marked our route up here like it was a four-lane highway."

Blake shivered. It had suddenly gotten a lot colder. "So who do you think they are?"

"Damned if I know. They're not tourists. And they're not friends of ours either, that's for damned sure... But it looks like they're on their way up here."

Blake sighed. "Jesus."

Winters got to her feet. "I'm going to check on Ray," she said. "And give him something to make him sleep." She walked off into the darkness toward the other tent, her flashlight a bright spark against the night.

"Okay," Blake said at last. "Maybe other people know the satellite came down somewhere in this part of the world. But we're supposed to be the only ones who know it's here, right? And yet they – or somebody – flew into Wambip just a day behind us. How do you figure that?"

"Somebody told them." Jeffries' face was a pale mask in the fireglow.

Blake looked toward the tent where Winters' light shone dimly through the fabric. "One of us?"

"How the hell should I know?" Jeffries said after a long moment. "But somebody told them." He took his gun out of his parka, looked at it for a moment, and put it back. "And that's why we're going up the wall tomorrow morning, Blake, without resting. To find the goddamned thing before they do."

* * *

Bent double in his sleeping bag, Blake listened to the whisper of the freezing wind as it ruffled the tent wall. In the endless blackness of the night, his eyes imagined strange shapes and colors, but his mind returned again and again to one image – that of the sheer rock wall they would climb tomorrow.

It would be easy, he knew, to slip quietly out of camp, to make his way into the forest and back down the trail to the village. Easy but dangerous. For there were men coming up that same trail now, men camped somewhere tonight on the ridge below them. Men who might pose even more of a threat to him than Jeffries.

And even if he escaped, what then? How long would it be before Sanford turned him in, and he'd have to run once more?

He opened the tent flap slightly and peered outside at the rock wall across the grasslands. There was no moon as yet; only the bright, terribly cold alpine stars hanging like ice diamonds in the blackness. On the ground, the night fog was slowly settling; in the morning, it would rise again, toward the peaks.

The cliff wall was a blank outline on the horizon, featureless and cold.

No running this time, he thought. All of them were together now, depending on each other for survival. The time for running was long gone. The time for fighting would come, as surely as the dawn.

All that mattered now was climbing the wall. Taking the next step.

He closed his eyes, exhausted. Fleeting glimpses of Winters' eyes and mouth drifted through his disconnected dreams as he slept fitfully in the cold and the silence, floating slowly toward morning and whatever the new day would bring.

# CHAPTER TEN

The fuel ignited with a small explosion, the stove roaring into life. Blake set the water on to boil and lay back in his sleeping bag, pulling it tight around him to keep the remaining shreds of warmth inside. In the glow of the hissing stove, the thermometer hanging from the tent wall read 30 degrees.

Beside him, Ed Jeffries stirred. "Christ, Blake. What time is it?"

"Just after four. Don't go back to sleep."

Jeffries' face appeared from the end of his down bag, red-rimmed eyes framed by dirty hair and a three-day growth of beard. "Go to hell," he muttered, brushing sleep from his eyes. "Why so damned early?"

Blake threw loose tea into the water and put the lid back on the pot. "Did you forget about the clouds? Sunrise is in an hour. By ten o'clock, the top of the wall will be socked in. We have to be off the rock face when that happens."

Jeffries grunted. "That doesn't give us much time, does it? Think we can get up the wall that fast?"

"I'll know as soon as it gets light," Blake said, handing him a cup of hot tea. "Now drink this and shut up."

* * *

At five-twenty exactly, the sun emerged over the horizon, flooding the grassy plateau with light. Blake picked up his binoculars and walked to the edge of the camp. Less than a mile away, the rock wall stood out clearly, sparkling in the morning sunlight and untouched as yet by mist or rain.

Blake felt satisfaction as he swept the glasses across the rock. Grey granite, just as he'd thought; perfect for climbing. In spite of himself, he felt the old excitement beginning to take hold inside his chest.

Jill Winters and Ed Jeffries appeared beside him, their breath making soft puffs of vapor in the thin morning air.

"It's damned cold up here," Winters said. "Quite a change from the rainforest, isn't it?"

"And it'll be colder up there," Blake said, gesturing with his glasses at the rock wall. "How's Corley this morning?"

"Much better. He's groggy and still complaining about a headache, but the swelling's gone from his ankle. I think he'll be all right."

Jeffries stared at the rock face. "Jesus, Blake," he muttered. "How the hell are we going to get up that thing? It looks almost straight up."

"It's not as hard as it looks," Blake replied. "And I think I've found a route up."

"A route? I don't see anything but sheer rock."

Blake handed him the glasses. "Look down there at the bottom," he said, pointing at the base of the wall. "See all that rock debris piled up there? That takes care of the first five hundred feet – it's nothing but a scramble. After that, there's a long crack going up at an angle. See it?"

Jeffries followed the crack with the glasses. "Yeah, I see it. It goes left, then right. Comes out on that ledge up there. You think we can we get up that okay?"

Blake nodded. "We'll have to rope together, but it should be safe enough. That ledge is at least a thousand feet up."

"But that's only halfway there," Jeffries pointed out. "What happens then?"

"Look to the right," said Blake. "There's a chimney – a wide crack – starting about fifty feet from where the ledge ends. It goes almost straight to the top. See it?"

Jeffries nodded.

"We'll go up that."

Jeffries studied the rock face for a few moments. Then he turned to Blake. "That chimney of yours finishes about a hundred feet from the top," he said. "After that, I don't see much. It goes straight up – no cracks, no ledges that I can see. How are we going to get up that?"

Blake took the glasses and scanned the clifftop carefully. "I'm not sure yet," he said at last. "But we'll find a way. We'll have to."

A shout came from behind them, and everyone turned to see Ray Corley stumping across the short grass, the radio transceiver in his hand. He puffed up to them, his hair sticking out in untidy clumps.

"Listen to this," he gasped. "It just came on." He held up the radio and turned up the gain.

> *...repeating our earlier bulletin: the Meteorological Service has issued an all-ships advisory effective at noon today for the waters of the Bismarck Archipelago and the Huon Gulf. A massive low front is approaching from the east. It is now over Bougainville and the Solomon Sea, and is moving steadily westward. It is expected to produce high winds and heavy rain during the next forty-eight hours in the waters and inland areas between Jayapura and Lae. All shipping is advised to seek safe harbor immediately. Repeat: all shipping is advised to seek safe harbor immediately.*
> *Returning now to our program of light music, here is the latest single from a group of...*

Blake reached over and snapped off the set. "It's the monsoon," he said, pointing to the clouds already edging up over the eastern horizon. "I figured we'd catch a storm sooner or later."

"They said the storm was to the east," said Jeffries. "Do you think we'll be affected?"

"Absolutely," said Blake. "It's moving west, and we're right in its path. It'll just take a while to get here, that's all."

Corley's eyes were wide. "How long?"

Blake shrugged. "Sometime tomorrow, I'd guess." He zipped up his parka. "We don't want to be on the rock face when it hits, that's for sure." He turned to Jeffries. "So you'll get your wish – we'll be going up the wall today."

\* \* \*

"Time to rope up," Blake said. They had stopped four hundred feet up the wall now, on the rock debris at the base of the cliff. The air was still and clear, the temperature brisk and invigorating. The crack they would climb struck off at an angle above them, wide and deep. So far, Blake could see plenty of good handholds. That was good; at least the first part would be easy.

"We'll only use one of our ropes for this part," he said. "I'll lead. Jill's second. Then Ed, and finally Ray. Everybody got their waist slings on? Good. Clip on, and let's get started."

Beside them lay the rucksacks containing the gear they would need to climb the wall, and afterwards, to survive on the ridge beyond. Two mountain tents, four days' supply of food, extra clothing, the radio sets and a first aid kit – all neatly packed away, divided among the four of them.

Blake had the heaviest load. In the pockets of his pack he had added the stove, two full bottles of fuel, and a packet of signal flares. Clipped to the outside of his pack was an assortment of climbing hardware – including slings, pitons, a rock hammer, chocks and carabiners, lengths of nylon parachute cord, and the extra climbing rope.

Blake talked quietly to the group as he checked and adjusted their slings. "We climb one at a time, in strict order. Nobody moves until the person in front has stopped and moved into a secure belay position. On each pitch I'll be going first. When I find a good place to stop, I'll belay Jill while she climbs up. Then both of us will belay Ed, and then finally Ray. Okay so far?"

At the sound of his name, Corley started guiltily. "Huh? What was that?" He stared vacantly at the group, squinting his eyes in the bright sunlight.

"Are you all right?" asked Winters.

"It's this damned headache," he mumbled. "Can't seem to get rid of it." He shook his head, sunlight glinting off his heavy spectacles. "I'll be okay in a while."

"Belaying is simple," Blake continued. "You take up slack on the rope as your partner climbs." He looped the climbing rope around his waist to demonstrate. "Once I get to the top of a pitch, I'll anchor myself to the rock with pitons, and then wrap the rope around myself as the next person starts to climb. There's a lot of friction on the rope, so it's easy to hold someone's full weight if necessary."

"Why?" Corley was staring at the rope.

"In case you fall, dummy," said Jeffries.

"That's right," said Blake patiently. "If someone slips or falls, the person belaying just has to tighten their grip on the rope, and they can arrest the fall. They'll only fall a few inches before the rope tightens up. You belay sitting down if you can, feet well braced. You wrap the rope around you for maximum friction. You'll be anchored to the rock with pitons, so that you can't be yanked off. Watch."

He demonstrated a sitting and a standing belay, showing them how to loop the rope around waist and shoulders. "You can hold someone with just one hand, if you've got enough friction. If—"

"Hold it." Jeffries cocked his head, listening. "Hear anything?"

Blake listened. A moment later, he heard the faint beating of rotors. "Helicopter," he said. "They're back. Everybody down, behind the rocks."

A moment later, they saw the Indonesian patrol helicopter appear up over the edge of the plateau. More than a mile away, it passed far to the south of them, headed off toward the border area at an angle.

They stayed behind the boulders until the noise of the rotors died away completely. "Son of a bitch," said Jeffries softly. "If they spot us while we're climbing, we've had it."

"Then we'd better get going," Blake said. "I'll say it again – we go up the rock in order, one by one. And we use spoken signals. Discipline on the rock is what saves your life, so remember what I'm telling you. Your partner will call out 'on belay' when it's safe for you to start. You yell 'climbing' when you start to move. That way everybody knows what's happening at all times. One person climbs at a time; everybody else stays right where they are. Then we set up a belay and the next person starts to climb. Got it?"

Corley shook his head. "What am I supposed to do?"

"Jesus. Weren't you listening?" Jeffries turned to him. "Just keep your mouth shut and watch the others, Ray, okay?" Then, to Blake, he said, "We can haul him up like a sandbag if we have to."

Blake agreed. Corley was the weak link; that was why he was last on the rope. He wouldn't have to belay anyone.

He put on his pack and checked the rope one last time. "Watch where I put my hands and feet," he told the others. "And try to do the same. I'll drive in pitons for safety – snap your carabiners off and back on again as you go up. Don't grab the pitons, and don't step on them – you might knock them out. Lean into the rock as you climb, and move only one hand or foot at a time." He looked up. "Ready? Climbing!"

Clanking, he hoisted himself smoothly into the start of the wide crack. It's almost wide enough to walk up, he thought with satisfaction. Effortlessly, he climbed fifty feet up, stopping when he found a perch where all of them could fit. He arranged himself in a sitting belay and called to Winters. A moment later he heard her cry of "climbing!"

As she worked her way slowly up the crack, he drew up the slack on the rope, glancing up at the clouds from time to time. They'd moved closer now, looking more massive than before. In a few hours – maybe less – they would cover the peaks.

A few moments later Winters sat beside him on the narrow ledge, her face flushed with excitement. He smiled at her. "Not so bad, was it?"

She looked down at the others, fifty feet below. "I'm just glad it's you, Peter, on the end of the rope."

Ten minutes later, Ed Jeffries arrived, breathing heavily. "Harder than it looks," he gasped.

"You're climbing too fast," Blake said. "The air's thin at this altitude. Make your movements short and economical, and rest every few minutes. We've got plenty of time; don't fight the rock."

"I'll be all right," Jeffries said curtly. He pointed to Corley below, struggling awkwardly up the rock. "But what about him? He seem a little funny to you this morning?"

"Let's hope he snaps out of it," said Blake.

Jeffries grunted. "Hope all you want. And watch him, in the meantime."

* * *

The cold air seemed to sparkle as Blake edged up the narrow crack, high up on the rock face. His entire body vibrated with that unique combination of physical and mental exhilaration that rock climbing can produce; the interweaving of intellect and instinct that made it possible for him to move up the rock like a spider, seemingly without effort.

Below him, the plateau shimmered gently in the sunlight. Heavy clouds were pouring up over the edge of the ridge at an accelerating rate, still far off but drawing ever closer. Plenty of time, he thought, hammering another piton into place and listening to it ring. Plenty of time. At this rate, they would be on top well before the clouds reached them.

He glanced down at the anxious faces crowded together on the narrow ledge below. Plenty of time, he corrected himself, unless something happens. Unless we have an accident.

\* \* \*

A grim-faced Jeffries clutched at the tiny handhold above him and tried hard not to move. "What the hell do we do now, Blake?" he said, his voice hoarse and strained. "You've been looking at that goddamned rock for ten minutes now."

Secured by pitons, the group huddled uncomfortably on the six-inch wide ledge and watched as Blake scanned the rock face with his binoculars. They perched at the top of the crack now, more than a thousand feet above the grasslands, just over halfway up, but fully exposed on the cliff face. Winters was doling out codeine tablets to Corley, whose headache had unaccountably worsened in the last hour.

We're too high for comfort now, Blake thought, and too exposed. They'd all been on the rock face too long. It was making everyone nervous. Time to get moving. The chimney that constituted a nearly direct route to the top of the wall began a mere fifty feet away, up slightly and to the right. To get there would require a fully exposed traverse across rock which offered only minimal holds. It could be done, he saw, but only with great care.

He put down his glasses. "Give me a few minutes to set the pitons," he said. "Once they're in, we should have no problem."

Winters turned to him, her face pale. "Peter, I'm getting frightened. There's nothing down there – nothing at all. It was all right before, but I'm scared now." Her voice rose, tinged with panic. "I– I can't climb across that, Peter. I just can't."

"Don't look down." Blake's voice was steady and strong. "Don't think about what's below. Keep your body close to the rock. You'll be on belay the whole time." He squeezed her shoulder and gave a small smile. "We'll be all right."

Then he began to climb.

He inched up and sideways, feeling cautiously for holds. Every few feet he hammered in a piton. At this rate, he thought, I'm going to run out of iron soon, but it can't be helped. They needed the extra margin that the pitons gave them. Especially because of Corley, who practically had to be dragged up the pitches bodily.

Halfway across now, another twenty feet to go to reach the chimney. He resisted the impulse to hurry. Don't fall, he told himself. Even though the pitons will catch you, you might crack a rib or pull a muscle. Worse than that, your falling would terrify the others, and they're already beginning to lose their nerve. Even Jeffries, the strongest of the group, was showing the strain.

So be very careful, he told himself, because this is the point of no return. If something happened to him now, he knew, the others would never be able to get off the rock face by themselves. And even if they tried, the clouds would probably catch them first, showering them with wind and freezing rain while their strength and their nerve leaked slowly away. Blake wiped sweat from his forehead and started across the last section of rock.

Moments later, he crouched safely inside the wide chimney. He anchored himself with a piton and waited a few moments for his breathing and his heartbeat to return to normal. When he was ready, he rose and called to Winters to come across.

"I'll have you on belay the whole way!" he shouted. "Remember, keep moving, and don't look down!"

Nodding grimly, she started across. He watched carefully as she inched across the sheer face, moving stiffly. Halfway. Three-quarters. Ten feet left to go.

Then she stopped. Spread-eagled on the rock, she froze. Blake could hear her ragged breathing, could almost feel the fear radiating from her.

"Keep moving, dammit!" he hissed at her. "It's only a few more feet."

"I– I can't find any more holds," she stammered. Her face was pinched with terror. "There's nothing. I can't move."

He felt sweat break out on his forehead. "There's a toehold to your right," he said. "About two feet away. Put your boot on it. It's down and to the right."

That was a mistake, he realized. Winters glanced down, and he heard her sharp intake of breath as she stared at the sheer drop-off below her. He saw her hands tighten on the rock.

"It's too small," she whispered. "I can't. I'll fall."

Blake gripped the rope and braced himself. He knew what was coming. "Try, Jill! It's safe, I've got you on belay! Now move!"

She shook her head, mute with fear, as she began to tremble violently. Here we go, he thought.

Her boots scraped loudly as she left the rock, and a single scream of pure terror came from her throat as she fell. The rope snapped against Blake with a shock and his body bent, absorbing the impact. Then she was dangling ten feet below him, crying softly.

"Safe now," he called to her. "It's over now, you're safe. I'm going to pull you up." Hauling on the rope with all his strength, he drew her up to him.

In his arms, she sobbed uncontrollably. He held her tightly and gentled her slowly, whispering reassurances to her.

"I was so frightened, Peter," she said between sobs. "So scared." Then she drew away, looking at him in surprise. "Peter, what's wrong? You're shaking even more than I am. Are you all right?"

He shook his head. "Delayed reaction, I guess." He got to his feet. "It's nothing. Let's get the others across. I'm fine."

That's a lie, he thought as he arranged the rope for Ed Jeffries. He wasn't fine at all. The image of Winters' face burned in his mind like the afterimage of a flashbulb. The way she had looked at him as she began to fall.

Exactly as Becky had looked at him. The day she had fallen to her death, so long ago.

# CHAPTER ELEVEN

The wind had picked up the last hour, the temperature dropping fast. Blake drew his parka tightly around him and blew on his hands to warm them. As he did, he glanced anxiously at the billowing clouds below. The mist was rising, faster than before. At this rate, it would reach them in about half an hour.

That's cutting it fine, he thought. Too fine. He swung his gaze back up to the rock above him. Time to get started.

They were all seated on a narrow ledge at the very top of the chimney, two thousand feet above the plateau. Miraculously, they had all made it across. They were all still alive. Below, the clouds had spread out across the entire horizon, creating the illusion of being suspended somewhere in time and space. Only the whistling of the wind gave proof that the world outside existed.

Exhaustion had etched itself deeply into their faces. Jeffries sat sideways on the ledge, his head between his knees. Winters gripped the rock tightly, her face turned away from the void below, her cheek pressed hard against the harsh comfort of the cold granite. Corley sat quietly, unmoving, his eyes staring vacantly at nothing at all.

Blake checked his equipment. He had few pitons remaining, and only half a dozen carabiners left. It'll have to be enough, he decided. They were so very close.

There remained a scant hundred feet of rock to climb. A hundred feet of sheer rock between them and the relative safety of the ridge at the top of the rock wall. We'll have to do this in one pitch, Blake decided. The group was disintegrating fast, their exhaustion fueled by mounting fear. They were down to the last reserves of their strength, he knew, and when that was gone, there would be no more.

So go straight to the top, he told himself. No staging; no belays. Get to the top and haul the rest of them up after you, one by one. All that matters now is getting off this damned rock face, and fast.

He turned to Winters. "Rope off."

"What?"

"Unhook your rope." He saw the fear on her face. "I'll make you secure to the rock with pitons," he added. "I need the extra rope length for this last part. If I take you off the rope, I'll gain another fifty feet to climb with. That should be enough to get me to the top."

"Isn't that dangerous, going all that way at once?"

"Not unless I fall. And I don't intend to fall. But," he added, "it would be better to have Ed belay me for this one, I think. He's stronger; got more weight."

Jeffries nodded. "You're right; I see what you mean. And it's the quickest way. If we don't get off this goddamn rock soon, the clouds will catch us. I don't know about the rest of you, but I don't feel like spending the night here, not when we're so close to the top." He got slowly to his feet. "Let's try it."

Five minutes later, Blake inched his way up the sheer face, moving like a spider in a slow-motion ballet. Jeffries belayed him from below as he climbed. Careful now, he told himself. One slip and you'll fall twice the length of the rope before Ed can catch you. So watch what you're doing.

Only a hundred feet to climb, he told himself. You've done this kind of thing dozens of times. Keep moving, don't look down, and don't think too much about anything. Just get there. He wiped sweat from his forehead with his free hand before hauling himself up another foot, his breath coming in short shallow gasps.

Now he was almost at the top, scant yards from the edge of the cliff. He rested a moment to let his dizziness subside. It's the damned altitude, he thought. We're nearly twelve thousand feet high. Don't look down, he reminded himself. Just keep going. Taking a deep breath, he began to inch forward.

Just then, he felt the rope go tight.

"More slack," he called down to Jeffries.

"Can't," came the reply from below. "You've got all the rope there is."

Cursing softly, Blake looked up. The top of the cliff lay perhaps ten feet above him now, certainly no more than twelve. Gripping the rock with frozen fingers, he swung out and back for a better look. A line of small but adequate holds ran straight up to the top from where he perched. He paused, considering.

"Jeffries," he called down a moment later. "I want you to climb up the rock a ways. I need about ten or fifteen feet of slack, that's all. Can you do that?"

There was a pause. "I don't think that's a good idea," Jeffries said at last. "There's not much to hang on to. And what about your belay?"

"Never mind the damned belay," Blake said impatiently. His fingers were starting to freeze. "It won't matter. I just need thirty seconds to get from here to the top, and I can't do that without some extra slack. And you've got good handholds, as far up as you need to come. Is everybody else okay?"

"Jill's off the rope, anchored tight into the rock. Corley's still tied on to the end of my rope. He's just sitting there."

"Then just climb on up. Ten or fifteen feet should do it."

Grunts and scraping noises came from below as Jeffries started up. A moment later, he said, "I can't go any further, Blake; this is the last good hold. I don't know how the hell you made it all the way up there, but this is the end of the line for me."

Blake eyed the slack rope. "This ought to do it," he said. "Just stay still and hang on. I'll be on top in just a minute."

"Peter, be careful." Winters' voice was tense.

"Not long now," he called back, reaching for the first hold. "Climbing!"

One step up. Two steps, three. A pause, while his fingers searched for the next knob of rock. His breath came in short, hard breaths, his nerve ends painfully sensitive as his feet and fingers explored the rock with tiny cautious movements, keeping him on a razor's edge of balance through friction and sheer willpower. Five feet to go.

From below, there came a hoarse shout.

Blake twisted around, looking down to see Jeffries, his face contorted with fear and anger, waving wildly at something just outside of Blake's line of vision. Birds? Insects? Snapping his head back the other way, he saw what had frightened Jeffries.

Corley had somehow unhooked himself from his piton anchor. Now he lurched drunkenly along the narrow ledge below Jeffries, his climbing rope still attached to his waist sling.

Jeffries' panic-stricken voice floated up to Blake, eighty feet above. "The stupid bastard's loose!" he shouted. "I can't reach him! What the hell is he doing?"

"Corley!" Blake screamed as loudly as he could at the figure on the ledge. "Corley, stop! Don't move!"

Corley seemed not to hear. One stumbling step at a time, he moved along the ledge toward Winters. The rope dangled down uselessly in front of him.

"Grab him, Jill!" Blake yelled. "Reach out and get him, for God's sake!"

Eyes wide with fright, Winters leaned forward, straining against the pitons which held her to the rock. As Blake watched, she stretched her arms as far as they would go toward Corley. He took a step closer; another few feet and she would have him.

Then he tripped. My God, thought Blake, he's going over.

Everything happened in horrific slow motion. As Winters began to scream, Corley toppled straight off the ledge, disappearing from sight. A second later, the rope linking Corley to Jeffries snapped taut, and then Jeffries, too, was falling, dragged over the side by Corley's weight and momentum.

Everything spun out of control now, the rope hissing wickedly as Jeffries plunged downward. Before Blake had time to react, a stabbing shock emptied his lungs of air, as he himself was pulled backward off the rock and began to fall. He opened his mouth to scream just as his head struck the rock face violently and a searing pain coursed through his chest.

When he regained consciousness, all downward motion had stopped. I'm still alive, he thought with amazement. I've stopped falling, and I'm still alive. His eyes dimmed with tears, and then, as sticky warmth began to spread, he realized that it was blood, not tears.

Wiping his face carefully with his sleeve, he looked up. His rope had caught on a protruding knob of rock some twenty feet above, and now he confronted every climber's ultimate nightmare. He was swinging from an unsecured rope, two thousand feet in the air, with no way for anyone to reach him.

The rope felt drum-tight around his chest. Below him, it swung slowly in the wind like a grisly pendulum, two motionless bodies hanging from its other end. Above him and somewhere off to the right, he could hear Jill Winters sobbing softly.

Then he became aware of movement.

The combined deadweight of the two bodies on the other end of the rope had become a counterweight, drawing him slowly upwards, toward the rock knob which had broken his fall. With dawning horror, Blake saw that once he reached the knob, the rope would slip off, and he would be dragged down the cliff.

Pain and shock were threatening to pull him back into unconsciousness. Fighting to keep his head clear, he looked desperately around him for handholds – cracks, knobs, anything to cling to. There were none.

Summoning up the last of his strength, he ground his palms into the rock, scraping the skin raw. It had no effect. He could slow himself fractionally, but he could not stop the inevitable upward movement. If he could only place a piton, he thought, he could stop the movement and stand some small chance of surviving. But to do that, the rope had to be slack. Inch by inch, he was being dragged upwards, toward the rock knob and disaster. He had only minutes to live.

"Jeffries! Jeffries, can you hear me?" Pain shot through his chest as he gasped out the words. "Answer me, for God's sake!"

A voice came faintly from below. "Blake! What the hell happened?"

"I don't know," Blake gasped. "Are you hurt badly?"

A pause. "Don't think so," Jeffries said at last. "Arm hurts, but I don't think it's broken. What are you doing up there? Why is the rope moving down?"

"Listen to me." Blake sucked in air and tried to speak as calmly as he could. "I'm hanging from a rock projection a few feet above me. Your weight is pulling me up toward it, and I can't stop the movement." He paused to take another deep breath. "What about Corley? Can you see him?"

"He's on the end of the rope," Jeffries replied. "About fifty feet below me. He isn't moving, Blake; just swinging there." A pause. "He looks dead. Jesus, Blake, what are we going to do?"

"I've got to stop the upward movement," Blake said. "If I can't, I'll be pulled off the rock. You've got to take the weight off somehow – just for a few moments. If you can do that, I can get a piton in... Otherwise, we're all going to fall."

There was no sound from below.

"Jeffries, can you hear me?"

"I hear you, dammit." Jeffries' voice sounded weaker than before. "I'm looking for footholds."

"Anything you can," Blake said. "Just get the weight off me."

"There's nothing." Jeffries' voice was panicky. "I don't– wait, there is something! A ledge, maybe three feet down. Just wide enough to stand on."

Blake wiped blood from his eyes and looked upward. Less than ten feet of rope remained now. For every inch he rose, Jeffries dropped the same amount. It might work, he thought.

His hands were beginning to freeze, the blood drying in cakes on his palms. He began to feel sleepy and numb from shock and exhaustion. It would be so easy, he thought, to just let go; to end the nightmare.

He shook his head. No, he told himself. You've got to try. Make it work. Because if it doesn't, you're all dead.

"Get ready," he shouted. "I'm dropping you down now."

Easing the pressure in his arms, Blake began to slide upward more quickly. Now he could no longer control his rate of movement. Two feet, three feet. Four. Jeffries, he thought, what the hell are you doing? What's happening down there? Less than five feet of rope left now.

He stopped moving.

"I'm on the ledge." Jeffries' voice came to him from far away. "Just a minute. I– there, I think it's okay now." A pause. "Christ, Corley's heavy. You'd better hurry up; I'm not sure I can hold him for long."

Now or never, Blake thought. Willing his arms and legs to function, he tugged at the rope, freeing it from the knob. Move fast, he told himself. Move fast, and don't slip.

With one hand, he found one of his remaining long pitons. Jamming it into a crack beside him, he groped for his hammer. He had perhaps sixty seconds – or less – to secure the two men below him. And at any moment, he knew, Jeffries could lose his toehold on the ledge.

He drove in the piton until it rang true, and then immediately placed another. Unsnapping the carabiner holding the climbing rope to his sling, he fashioned a double knot in the rope around the carabiner and clipped it through the large rings in the pitons he had just placed. Crude, he thought, but it'll do the job.

"For the love of God." Jeffries spoke in an exhausted whisper. "I'm slipping. Oh, please–"

"It's all right!" Blake shouted down. "You're anchored now! Let go if you have to!"

Holding his breath, he watched as the rope tightened, taking the full weight of the two men. The pitons held.

For the moment, they were safe.

Relief broke over him like an ocean wave, and he gripped the rock tightly to keep from fainting. Winters' voice came dimly through his tears and nausea. "Peter! What's happening? Are you all right?"

He nuzzled the cold rock with his cheek and closed his eyes. "I'm okay," he whispered. "We're all okay now."

His voice was lost against the keening of the wind.

# CHAPTER TWELVE

"You have any idea what the hell happened down there?" Blake watched Jeffries' face carefully as he asked the question.

The big man shivered, his hand going to his eyes. "Damned if I know," he said after a moment. "I'd just come up to that small ledge, giving you slack like you told me to." His eyes squinted as he remembered. "I found a handhold – just a nub of rock, really – and I stopped climbing." He turned to face Blake. "Then I heard Corley moving, down below me."

The two men sat huddled together at the top of the rock wall, staring down into the cloud-filled abyss below. The wind was fiercer, the air noticeably colder. The first tendrils of the rising mist had found them now, gusting up from below.

Blake had managed to drag them up past the overhang, onto the top of the rock wall. All of them collapsed in a heap behind one of the boulders, shivering in the cold and wind, while they recovered from the terror of the ascent. Eventually, Blake and Jeffries got to their feet and unpacked the two mountain tents. Fifteen minutes later, both tents were up. They dragged Corley into one of them, and Winters dug out her first aid kit and crawled inside with him to see what she could do.

Blake's altimeter read just over twelve thousand feet. Behind them, the ridge leading to Antares's summit snaked away to the west. We've got to be close to the nose cone now, Blake thought. He turned, conscious of the soreness in his ribs, and peered up the ridge. The summit of Antares was covered with clouds now, and it would stay that way until tomorrow morning. The moisture-filled clouds below them were rising, driven by the increasing wind. The temperature was already just below freezing, and that meant snow, and soon.

Once the clouds covered them completely, Blake knew, there would be whiteout conditions until tomorrow morning. He fumbled under his down vest and pulled out the heavy metal compass he carried on a rawhide thong around his neck. The compass was bulky, but it was special; Becky had given it to him for his birthday. "You'll never be lost with this," she'd said as she put it around his neck. "And it will always bring you back to me."

He leveled it and took several quick sightings up the ridge, filing the information away mentally for tomorrow.

On the map, it looked like easy going – three or four miles of approach along a gently-sloping ridgeline, with a total rise in altitude of less than two thousand feet. But the map doesn't take into account the approaching monsoon, thought Blake. Nor the half-dead man in the tent across the ledge in front of him.

He turned back to Jeffries. "You heard Corley below you," he repeated. "What happened then?"

"I looked down and saw that the bastard had unclipped himself. He was free and clear of the piton anchor, and moving – stumbling, really – along the ledge." He shook his head. "Goddamned if I know what he was trying to do. I shouted at him, but he didn't seem to hear... Then he tripped on the rope and fell."

Blake gazed back at the tent where Winters was trying to make Corley comfortable. It had taken all of them half an hour to drag Corley up the cliff face through the rising mist, and when they finally got him up over the lip, he was unconscious. Trembling with exhaustion, they had rigged their tents and bundled him inside one, wrapping him in sleeping bags against the bitter cold.

Winters crawled out of the tent and zipped it tightly shut. She walked over to stand beside them, her face drawn and anxious.

"You'd better come and look at Ray," she said to Blake in a quiet voice.

Inside the tent, Corley lay like a corpse, his face the color of raw putty. Blake noted a compress covering a bad gash on his cheek which he must have gotten during his fall. "Concussion?" he asked Winters.

"I don't think so. His pulse is weak, but the pupils are normal." She bit her lip. "I don't know what's wrong with him, frankly. He was awake a few moments ago, complaining of a terrible headache. Said it felt like his brains were about to explode. I gave him more codeine and made him drink some water. Then he started coughing."

She held up a handkerchief flecked with pink froth. "He's coughing up blood, Peter."

He snatched the handkerchief from her and examined it, a terrible suspicion looming in his mind. "Oh, hell," he breathed. "I should have known."

"What is it?"

"Hypoxia. Altitude sickness. I should have spotted it before – all the symptoms were there. Sleepiness, headache, irrationality. If he's started bringing up blood, it's serious." As he spoke, Corley began coughing again, shifting restlessly in his drugged sleep.

Jeffries peered into the tent at the sick man. "I don't get it. None of the rest of us are sick. Why just him?"

Blake shrugged. "Everyone reacts differently. We all had headaches and dizziness earlier, remember? That's a normal reaction to high altitude at first, but most people adapt in a day or so. Some don't. Corley didn't."

"Can we give him anything for it?"

"There's nothing much you can do for hypoxia," Blake said. "Drugs like Pervitin or Maxidon help temporarily, but we don't have either one."

"So what happens next? How long will it take him to pull out of it?"

Blake shook his head. "I don't think he will pull out. If he's coughing blood, it means he's well into the critical stage. His lungs are hemorrhaging. Eventually, he'll drown in his own blood."

Winters leaned forward. "Peter, isn't there anything we can do?"

"We have to bring him down," Blake said. "Get him to a lower altitude as fast as we can. Get him back to Wambip, and call for a plane to evacuate him. He might recover if we can do it fast enough."

Jeffries stared at him. "Are you crazy, man? Go back down, after all we've just been through? We're almost on top of the nose cone now – it can't be more than a few miles away at the most! It's out there, Blake, and I mean to find it. We're not leaving until we do. We'll go down then, not before."

Blake kept his voice even. "Maybe you don't understand. Corley hasn't just got a bad headache – he's going to die unless we do something." He gestured at the tent walls, whipping back and forth in the icy wind. "It's too late to start back today, but tomorrow morning we can probably get down the rock face if we start early enough."

He moved to Corley's pack and opened it. "I'm calling Mount Hagen on the radio, right now. With luck, we can have a helicopter waiting at the Wambip airstrip tomorrow afternoon." He pulled out the radio. "Trip's over, Jeffries."

Jeffries took the gun from his parka. Now he spoke in a low, dangerous voice. "Stay away from the radio, Blake. We're not stopping now – not for just one sick man!"

Blake ignored him. "Go to hell, Jeffries," he said calmly. He began removing the radio from its case. "If Ray stays up here, he'll die. And if he dies, you'll lose any hope of disarming the nose cone and getting the data module out of it." He freed the radio and snapped it on. Dials glowed and pointers twitched. "If Ray gets better, we can try again. But right now, he's dying."

Winters put her hand on Jeffries' arm. "He's right, Ed. Let him call. It's finished now."

Blake spun the vernier until he caught the carrier wave. Over it came a burst of static, and then a voice in heavily accented English began to recite Civil Defence call letters.

"Another thing," said Blake, raising his voice above the wind and the static. "Shoot me now, and you'll have no hope of ever getting down from here. You'd be dead right now if it hadn't been for me, and you'll be dead tomorrow if you try getting down that cliff on your own." His eyes met Jeffries'. "Think about it, Ed."

The gun wavered and finally came down. Jeffries' eyes burned with anger and frustration. "Call, then, you bastard," he muttered.

Blake picked up the microphone and thumbed the 'transmit' button, reading from the printed card taped to the side of the set. "Calling Civil Defence VJ8EA Mount Hagen. Civil Defence VJ8EA Mount Hagen, over."

Nothing. The dials glowed and the pointers quivered, but no response came from the tiny speaker. He tried again. "Calling Civil Defence, calling Civil Defence." There was desperation in his voice now. "Mayday, Mayday! This is an emergency! Please come in!"

The set hummed, but nothing happened. He tried again. And again.

Cursing, Blake snapped the set off and loosened the thumbscrews holding the back plate in place. Pulling out the transmitter module, he stared in horror at the maze of broken metal that appeared.

The back of the circuit board had been sabotaged: the cut ends of the wires still gleamed brightly. The receiver circuits were still intact, but the rest was a broken ruin.

There was silence in the tent as they all stared at the set and then at each other.

Blake's eyes swept over Ed Jeffries, Jill Winters, and the comatose Ray Corley. One of them did this, thought Blake. But who? And more importantly, why?

# CHAPTER THIRTEEN

The hands on Blake's watch read six o'clock. Morning again, he thought as he lay in his sleeping bag and shivered. Outside, the wind whistled savagely around the tent, popping the thin fabric of the walls like gunshots. The thermometer beside him read twenty-nine degrees. It would be colder outside, he knew.

The mountain stove hissed in the corner and their small gas lantern cast strange misshapen shadows as Blake and Jeffries moved sluggishly to prepare tea. As he sipped the scalding beverage, Blake looked at the equipment piled at the end of the tent. They would need to eliminate every ounce of unnecessary gear this morning before they attempted to descend the wall. They'd abandon the tents, extra clothing, and any climbing equipment they didn't need. They'd only carry some food and basic essentials – whatever was necessary for survival – on the trip back to Wambip village. They would need to start within the hour, Blake reckoned, to be sure of getting off the wall before the storm hit them.

His gaze shifted to the radio beacon and the box of emergency flares. He'd take them as far as the plateau, he decided, and dump them there once they re-entered the rainforest, on their way down to the village. They might be useful for signaling a passing aircraft, but only in an absolute emergency. The only aircraft likely to be in the area would be those of the Indonesian border patrols.

Jeffries broke the silence. "How are we going to get Ray down the wall?" He spoke quietly, with no trace of yesterday's anger in his voice.

"We'll have to rig a sling," said Blake, indicating the rope and climbing hardware. "Once he's tied in, we'll lower him down. It'll be slow-going." He checked his watch. "If we work quickly, and we don't have any accidents, we can probably be down on the plateau by noon. Then we'll make a hammock for him out of bamboo poles and start down the ridge. We could be in Wambip late this evening, if nothing else goes wrong."

Jeffries grimaced. "If nothing else goes wrong."

The tent flap opened, letting in a burst of icy air. "Is that tea I smell?" Jill Winters' face was grimy and her eyes were red-rimmed and puffy with exhaustion. "I didn't hear the breakfast gong."

Blake smiled at her and held out his mug. "We were just about to announce the first seating. Take this and come inside – you're letting all the warmth out."

When she was seated, he said, "How's Ray this morning? Any better?"

She shook her head. "Much the same as yesterday. Maybe a bit worse." She brushed hair from her eyes. "He's still coughing a lot. Bringing up more blood from time to time. It sounds horrible – all sort of bubbly."

"We'll start back as soon as we've finished this," Blake told her. "He might improve, once we get down below eight or nine thousand feet."

She glanced at the two men. "Have either of you been outside yet?" They shook their heads. "Then there's something you should see. Come on."

Holding her mug carefully, she crawled out of the tent. Shrugging on their parkas, Blake and Jeffries followed her.

The strong morning light made him blink, and the force of the cold wind hit him with a slap as he stood up and looked around him. It had gotten quite a bit colder outside, Blake decided. Ducking back into the tent, he rummaged in the packs, emerging a few moments later with three pairs of heavy insulated overmitts.

"Put these on," he directed as he passed them out. "With this wind, we've got a nasty wind chill factor. Keep them on at all times. Otherwise, you'll get frostbitten in a matter of minutes."

With his mittens on and his hood up, Blake looked around at his surroundings for the first time. Their camp lay on a wide flat spur of Antares's summit ridge. The jagged ridge stretched away from them to the northwest, curving slightly and rising as it approached the squat granite triangle of the summit.

To the left, south of the summit, bare rock plunged steeply down into the glacial valley he remembered from the aerial photographs they had examined in Mount Hagen. The scarp, dotted with tiny waterfalls and old avalanche scars, fell almost four thousand feet before meeting the bottom of the valley and the river that eventually found its way eastward through the jungle, back to the village of Wambip.

Winters lifted her gloved hand and pointed. "There," she said. "I saw it up there, just below the peak and to the left. Do you see what I'm pointing at?"

There on the bare rock, a dirty orange smudge was clearly visible. Blake raised his binoculars, his mouth dry with anticipation. There was no doubt about it, he thought, as the image jumped clearly into focus.

It was the nose cone's drag parachute.

The blue markings on the fabric were visible as the wind billowed and whipped the chute about. Blake could see shock cords leading from the chute to something hidden behind a jumble of boulders.

He passed the glasses to Jeffries. "It's the nose cone, all right," he said. "Right there in front of us. We'd have seen it yesterday if the mist hadn't come up so quickly."

Jeffries took a long look, his face tense with excitement. "Right under our goddamned noses," he breathed. "How far away do you think it is?"

"Distances are tricky at high altitudes," said Blake. "But it's probably not more than a couple of miles from here."

Jeffries passed the glasses to Winters. "Then we'll go for it."

Blake swung around, scanning the eastern horizon, a frown on his face. "Those thunderheads out there are headed straight for us, and fast," he said. "The monsoon's going to pass directly over us in a couple of hours."

"So we get some rain," said Jeffries. "We can handle that. I say we get moving."

"Not rain," said Blake. "It'll be snow. Snow, ice and freezing temperatures." He swept the lowering sky slowly with the binoculars. "If we go after the nose cone, we'll be stuck up here until after the storm blows itself out. Twenty-four hours at least." He swung to Jeffries. "I don't think Ray can last that long, frankly. I still say we go down. Right now."

Jeffries' eyes flashed. As he opened his mouth to speak, Winters laid a hand on his arm. She had been scanning the plateau below them.

"Look," she said in an urgent voice. "Down there. Just at the edge of the forest."

Blake swung the glasses down. On the *kunai* plateau two thousand feet below, something was moving.

He focused with clumsy fingers, and now he could see them clearly. Two men, coming out of the rainforest on the far side of the *kunai*. On the same path they themselves had used. As he watched, they came quickly out from under the trees, heading across the flat plain. They carried climbing packs, with what looked like ropes and long ice axes strapped to the outside.

"What the hell are you two looking at?" Jeffries' voice intruded abruptly.

Blake passed him the glasses. "We've got visitors," he said. "Heading straight toward our base camp. They must be the two we saw the other day, getting off that plane at Wambip."

Jeffries swore softly. "I think you're right," he said after a moment. "Son of a bitch. They're about two miles away, and coming fast." He swung back toward Antares's summit, looking again at the spot where the drag parachute flapped and billowed in the rising wind. "How long, Blake? How long do you figure it would take us to get up to the nose cone? Could we make it before the storm arrives?"

Blake stared at him. "I thought we'd decided, Jeffries. We're going down, not up."

Jeffries grasped him by the front of his parka. "Goddamnit, Blake. You think those are tourists down there? Daytrippers? Or maybe the US Cavalry, come to save us? They're after the nose cone, just like us!" He brought his face close to Blake's, the words hissing out in an angry stream from between his clenched teeth. "We've left a trail of climbing iron on that wall that a blind man could follow. They can be here in a few hours, Blake, and when they get here, they'll look for us first."

"Us? Why?"

Jeffries gestured to the tent where Corley lay. "Because Ray's the only one who knows how to disarm the module, dammit! They're going to hunt us down, Blake." He turned toward Antares. "We've got to get out of here. And there's only one way left to go."

Blake looked at the ridge. "You're crazy," he said softly. "Crazy. We'll never be able to do it."

Winters shook her head. "I think Ed's right," she said quietly. "It may be our only chance. Like you said, the storm's going to come up fast. We've got to move. If we stay here, we're in real trouble."

Jeffries pointed south, down into the glacial valley and the river glinting far below. "It should only take a couple of hours to get to the nose cone and detach the module.

Then, instead of coming back this way, we'll go down the other side. It's longer, but they'll never find us. We can use our climbing ropes to drop straight off the crest, straight down into the valley there. We'll hide in the forest, follow the river back to Wambip. We can do it, Blake. When the storm hits, they'll be up here, and we'll be down there."

His breath rasped in the thin air. "Think about it. If we come back with the data module, you're in the clear, and all of us are rich. But if we go back down that wall now, we're all dead." He paused. "It's all we've got, Blake."

It might just work, Blake thought, sweeping his eyes over Antares's summit again. It might just be possible. Everything depended on getting to the nose cone and down into the depths of the valley before the storm unleashed its fury. Before the clouds blanketed the peak.

It would be a race against time. If they lost, they would be immobilized, trapped on a mountaintop with a dying man. And their pursuers would be there with them, playing a deadly game of hide-and-seek.

He raised his glasses again and trained them on the grassy plateau. The two men were nearer now, walking quickly one behind the other through the short *kunai* grass. Their image appeared sharp and clear in the lenses; Blake could even see the puffs of condensation from their breathing as they marched along.

They were white men, he saw; both of them looking highly professional in their climbing boots, windbreakers and high-altitude goggles. They moved quickly and without apparent effort, despite their packs being loaded with equipment.

He stopped breathing as he focused on what was strapped to their backpacks. What he had taken to be ice axes weren't ice axes at all.

They were automatic rifles.

He looked at Jeffries, who nodded. "I saw it too," he said. "If you're satisfied now, we'd better break camp and get moving. We haven't got much time."

# CHAPTER FOURTEEN

"It's no use," Winters said in a weary voice. "Why don't we just admit it? It's not going to work."

She glanced at Corley's body, lying on the cold ground beside her, and then back up at the peak. The orange chute billowed in the near distance, just below the summit. "We're closer," she said, "but it might as well be a million miles from here. If only he could walk."

Defeated, they sprawled on the bare rock, sheltered from the wind behind some boulders. Their faces were burned raw from the wind and the sun, their eyes dark and sunken with fatigue. As they drank their tea, their breathing came in short, shallow gasps. The altitude was affecting everyone, Blake knew. There simply wasn't enough oxygen in the air. It was cold, they were exhausted, and one slip might send someone sliding over the edge. To either side of them, the rock dropped away steeply, down into the rainforest thousands of feet below. Ahead, the summit loomed up behind a sharp overhang, dark and forbidding.

Blake took off his glove and ran his fingers over the stubble on his face. Gingerly, he felt the crusted blood covering the wide gash on his forehead. He put his glove back on, flexing his fingers to restore the feeling. His hand had only been exposed to the wind for a few seconds, but already his skin had started to freeze.

"Well, he can't walk," he said in a tired voice. "He's barely conscious, in fact. And there's no way in hell we're going to get him up that." He trained the binoculars up on the rock overhang which barred their way.

They'd broken camp hours earlier, moving like zombies as they folded their tents and stowed them in their packs. Breathing was a trial, and everyone had to pause every minute or so to catch their breath and recover a bit of energy. Finally they'd been ready, and so they set out along the summit ridge, Blake in the lead, shuffling like prisoners in some high-altitude winter gulag.

So far, despite their exhaustion, progress up the ridge had been slow but steady, one foot in front of the other. Blake and Jeffries had supported Corley between them as they staggered along. Now the overhang made forward progress impossible. It jutted up sharply from the narrow ridge crest, less than a hundred feet high; a freak fault breaking an otherwise gentle rate of climb. Beyond, the ridge appeared to continue without difficulty, straight to Antares's summit and the parachute which lay just below it.

It was possible to climb the overhang, Blake knew. But not if Corley had to be hauled along. Given enough time and strength, they could probably manage it. But time and strength were gone now, all used up.

Jeffries stared at the clouds behind them. "Storm's coming up behind us faster than we thought," he murmured. "Those clouds are almost here."

"Moving fast," Blake said. "We'll be socked in within the hour." He sniffed the air. "Snow's coming, too, probably."

Winters shivered in her down parka. "It's getting colder," she said. "Well, what are we going to do? If we just stay here, we'll freeze."

Blake looked again at the overhang. The rock slope reared up sharply just in front of them and then curved back on itself, just a few feet from the top. Blake cursed inwardly. Getting up the first part would be relatively easy, he thought. But negotiating the overhang would be another matter altogether.

"There's only one way to manage this," he said at last. "We'll have to haul him up in a sling." He looked over at Corley, now lying flat on the ground behind the rocks. "Is he conscious?"

"In and out," replied Winters. "Why?"

"He needs to understand what we're going to do. He needs to keep a grip on the rope for this to work."

Walking over to Corley, he knelt and began to speak, slowly explaining what was going to happen. Corley seemed to be listening, but made no sign. Once or twice, his eyes flickered.

"Just a few more hours," Blake concluded, "and we'll have you off the mountain. Just as soon as we've extracted the data module from the nose cone. We're very close."

Corley lay silent when he had finished, his eyes focused on some distant point in space. His voice, when it finally came, was paper-thin and infinitely tired. A dry whisper, barely audible against the keening wind.

One word. "No."

Blake grasped his shoulders gently. "Ray, listen to me," he said. "The men who are following us will kill us if they find us. We're almost on top of the nose cone now, and you're the only one of us who can disarm the thing. You've got to try, man. It's our only chance."

Silence, and then Corley spoke again. "You don't understand," he whispered. "I'm dying."

Jeffries stood behind Blake. "You're not dying, dammit," he said. "You've just got altitude sickness. Once we get off the mountain, you'll be fine."

Corley shook his head and began coughing, bringing up a large quantity of bright red foam. Blake took the man in his arms, cradling him like a small child, trying to quiet the spasm. The coughing lasted several long minutes, and when it was finally over, Corley spoke again.

"Altitude sickness? Maybe. But I've also got a bad ticker. Congestive heart disease. And it's going to kill me."

Jeffries stared at him. "Bullshit. I've read your file inside and out. There's nothing in it about heart disease!"

Corley smiled faintly. "I hope not. I made damned sure it never got into my file, Ed. One more year with Boomer and I could have retired on pay." He coughed again. "Too bad it didn't work out. Private doctor in Washington diagnosed me a couple of years ago. Gave me some kind of digitalis thing for it, told me to take it easy. As long as I take the pills, I'm okay."

Winters leaned forward. "Where are the pills, Ray?"

"Gone," Corley whispered. "All gone. They were in my pocket when I fell. They're gone now. They fell out; I saw them go."

"Christ!" Jeffries exploded. "Of all the—"

"Wait." Corley held up a trembling hand. "Listen to me." He coughed again. "You don't need me to recover the data module. You never did. You can do it yourselves." His eyes shifted sideways. "My pack, in the bottom. The flat metal box."

Winters quickly found the box and passed it to him. Hands shaking, Corley pried off the top. Inside was a folded piece of cloth, and inside that, a thin strip of metal six inches long. Grooves ran along its length.

Corley handed it to Jeffries. "It's an electronic key, Ed. This is all you need. This and the code. This will disarm the explosive. Take it."

He wiped blood from his mouth before continuing. "This was my insurance policy, see? With Boomer. With Sanford, too. It meant they couldn't just cut me out of things... They're both evil bastards, just in different ways."

He took a long wheezing breath. "Guess it didn't work that well, did it? So now you get to do it on your own." His voice had dropped again, and Blake bent forward to hear him.

"The key is electronically matched to magnetic patterns in the self-destruct unit," he whispered. "Just insert it and turn. The countdown sequence starts and you have forty-five seconds to input the code. That disarms the bomb and unlocks the module."

"Insert it where?" Jeffries' eyes were bright.

"There's an inspection hatch. On the side of the nose cone, outlined in white. Open that first. The data module is inside, recessed into the bulkhead. Next to it is a slot marked 'Auto-Destruct'. Put the key in there and turn it. Type in the code and wait until the lights turn green. Then you can slide the module out."

"What code?"

"Around my neck."

Blake fumbled under the man's shirt and drew out a laminated card on a lanyard. On the card was printed a string of numbers.

"You've got forty-five seconds. After that, the thing blows up."

Jeffries stood up. "Why didn't you tell us all this earlier, you sonofabitch?"

Corley stared back at him, his eyes vulnerable without their thick glasses. "Told you, Ed. I didn't trust Amos Sanford." He coughed. "Hell, I don't trust you, either, come to that. But it doesn't matter anymore now, does it?"

"Forget all that," Blake said. "We're wasting time." He looked around, scanning the ground around them. "We'll set up the tents behind those boulders over there. Put Ray in one of them and cover him with sleeping bags. He'll be safe until we get back."

"And if they find him?" Jeffries said.

Blake shook his head. "I don't think they will. This area will probably be whited-out within the hour." He reached inside his shirt and drew out the heavy compass that hung on its rawhide thong. "We'll take compass bearings to find our way back here."

"I should stay," Winters said. "Ray's going to need someone to look after him."

"No," said Blake. "You're coming with us. There's really nothing you can do for him here. If anything happens up on the summit, we'll be better off with three people."

He glanced at the darkening sky; already the first few flakes of snow were falling. "You and Jill get the tents set up," he said to Jeffries. "I'll pack some survival gear for us and take the initial bearings. Once we recover the module, we'll use the same bearings to get here and drop down into the valley. Even with heavy cloud cover, we should be able to make it."

Jeffries looked down the steep slope, already filled with mist. "But we won't be able to see where the hell we're going, will we?"

"We're only going in one direction," Blake replied shortly. "Straight down. The alternative is to ride out the storm up here on the ridge, with a dying man and a couple of killers with automatic rifles."

Jeffries spat. "Not too many options, are there?"

Blake pulled up the hood on his parka. "None," he said. "Not anymore."

The snowflakes, thicker now, danced past them on the wind.

"Let's get started," Blake said. "Every second counts now."

# CHAPTER FIFTEEN

Jill Winters and Ed Jeffries sat at the top of the overhang, gasping for breath, watching as Blake drove in the anchor pitons. Below them, the rising clouds had already obscured the two tents they had left behind. The storm front moved across the mountain, whipping large flakes of snow past them as the day grew darker and colder by the moment.

Blake stood up. "It's secure," he shouted over the wind's roar. Hands encased in bulky overmitts, he fumbled with the climbing ropes, tying them together and feeding one end through the carabiner attached to the anchor pitons. He let go of the rope and it snaked away down the cliff, disappearing into the whiteness below.

"We'll use this to rappel down again," he said. "Once we get back down to the bottom, we'll pull the rope back through the carabiner and recover it. We'll use the same method for getting off the ridge and down into the valley afterwards. I reckon we've got just enough climbing hardware to make it."

He turned to look at the summit. Snow had already covered the bare rock, transforming the ridge into a featureless white world, without shadows or landmarks. It would be all too easy, he knew, to become lost now, within sight of their goal.

He took a length of nylon parachute cord from his pack. "We'll rope together now, with this. Parachute cord won't stop a fall, but it'll keep us together and moving in the same direction. I'll be navigating by compass from now on. In a few minutes we won't be able to see more than a few feet in any direction."

He made the cord secure to each of them, clipping it on to their sling belts. "Single file now," he said. "Ed behind me, Jill behind Ed. I'll call out the compass bearings every thirty yards or so. One foot at a time, very slowly. And watch your step – it's getting damned icy."

* * *

Fifteen minutes later, Blake felt a tug on the cord. Brushing snow from his goggles, he stopped and turned. He was barely able to make out the shape of Jeffries as he crouched over Winters, bent down in the snow.

"What's the problem?"

Winters' white-rimmed face turned up to face him. "My boot lace came loose. Give me a minute; I want to tighten it."

"Hurry up," said Blake. "The storm's picking up."

Nodding, Winters bent to her task, removing her gloves and setting them beside her. Blake looked around at the driving snow, listening to the scream of the wind as it pushed against him. Reaching inside his parka, he took out the heavy compass and checked his bearing again. Straight ahead, he thought with satisfaction. Very close. Less than a mile away now.

Then he heard Winters' cry of alarm.

Turning, he saw her make a desperate grab for something, miss, and nearly fall. He ran back to where she and Jeffries stood staring down the steep ridge, into the whirling snow.

"What happened? Are you all right?"

"She's lost her goddamned gloves," Jeffries snapped. "Wind picked them up and took them over the edge, before either of us could react."

"It happened so fast." Winters' face was stricken. "What do we do now?"

Blake stared into space, considering. The wind chill factor was close to zero now, he calculated. Exposed flesh would start to freeze in minutes. They had no spare gloves, nothing to cover her hands with.

He cursed inwardly, blaming himself. He should have been prepared for this; it happened even with professional climbers. There was nothing they could do now, he realized; she couldn't keep on without gloves, and it was too late to try to get her back to camp.

"You'll have to stay here," he said finally. "Put your hands inside your parka, up into your armpits, and keep them there. I'll wrap you up in the emergency bivvy sack." He looked around, spotting the grey outline of a clump of boulders off to the side. "Help me get her set up over there, Ed."

Jeffries nodded, brushing thick flakes of wet snow from his eyebrows.

Blake pulled out the emergency bivouac bag from his pack, along with a lightweight foil space blanket. They wrapped Winters tightly in both and nestled her in behind the rocks. The rocks are poor shelter from the biting wind, thought Blake, but better than being fully exposed in the open. Breathing hard in the thin air, the two men made her as comfortable as possible.

"It's so cold," she murmured in a voice barely audible against the wind.

Blake poured hot tea from his thermos and gave it to her, putting the rest beside her. "Here's some chocolate, too," he said. "Eat it quickly and get your hands under cover. You need to keep them warm at all costs." He looked at his watch. "We'll be back in an hour, maybe less. Don't move from here." He tapped his compass. "I've got a bearing on you now. If you move, we might not find you again."

She smiled faintly. "I'm not going anywhere." Her eyes met Blake's and her fingers, icy cold, brushed his cheek. "Hurry back, Peter. And for God's sake, be careful."

\* \* \*

123

They trudged slowly through the snow, pausing every few steps to gasp for air and to rest their exhausted muscles. It can't possibly be much further, thought Blake for perhaps the tenth time. Unless we've missed it. If we've already passed the nose cone without knowing it, we could walk forever.

Under their feet, the snow was now two inches thick and building up with every passing second. Blake trudged along, his apprehension growing with every passing moment. The expedition has been a terrible mistake, he thought. We never should have attempted this, not with untrained people. Another accident is only a matter of time. And when that happens, he thought, it'll be each to their own.

Brushing snow from his goggles, he took another step forward, found his feet tangled in something, and fell heavily into the snow. Behind him, Jeffries gave an excited shout. Ribs grinding painfully, he got to his feet, untangling them from the shrouds of a bright orange parachute.

They had found the nose cone.

Wordlessly, both men began brushing snow away from the grey-black object attached to the parachute. Moments later, it lay fully exposed before them.

Blake stared, unable to believe his eyes. It was exactly as he imagined it: a squat cone about ten feet long, matte black and grey, with white stenciled markings. Near the broad base, a small American flag and the words 'ENVISION ENTERPRISES LTD' had been partially burned away by the heat of re-entry.

Jeffries stepped back to look at it. "Ugly thing, isn't it?" he said. "Looks more like a bomb than a rocket."

Blake looked up. "It is a bomb," he said. "The data module has a self-destruct mechanism, remember? It'll probably kill us both if we set it off."

They walked slowly around it until they came to an inspection hatch outlined in white.

"There it is," said Jeffries. "Just like Ray said" – he leaned forward – "but how the hell do we get it open?"

Blake looked and saw four flat screws holding the hatch in place. "I can get a piton blade in there, I think," he said finally. "But are you sure it won't blow up if we touch it?"

Jeffries took a deep breath. "No, I'm not sure," he said. "But does it make any difference at this point?"

Blake smiled grimly and reached for his pack. "Right," he said.

The snow fell thickly around them as he fitted a knife piton into the first of the recessed slots with trembling hands. He held his breath and turned the first screw.

Then the second. And the third and fourth. With a soft plop, the hatch fell off in his hands. In spite of the cold, both men were sweating now as they bent to peer inside.

Snapping on his flashlight, Blake could make out a maze of wires and printed circuits. Behind a bank of microchips, he saw a plate of shiny metal with two small handles and the words 'Data Module' stenciled across the top.

"That's it," whispered Jeffries. "That's it!"

"Easy," Blake warned. "Look there." He pointed above the module to a small slot marked 'Auto-Destruct'. A death's head and the warning 'Danger High Explosive' were prominently displayed beside it. Underneath it was a small keyboard and a set of indicator lights. "Got the key?"

"Cross your fingers." Jeffries slid the end of the metal key into the slot and turned it. The indicators lit up, blinking red, and a shrill beeping began, coming from somewhere inside the mechanism. With trembling, freezing fingers, he typed in the code printed on Corley's laminated card.

The beeping continued.

"What the hell?"

Blake took off his glove, reached past Jeffries, and hit 'enter' on the keyboard. The beeping stopped.

The two men looked at each other.

"Well, shit," Jeffries said after a long moment. "Think it's safe now?"

"Only one way to find out," said Blake. He gave a sharp tug on the metal handle. It came out easily.

The module was grey flat metal, eighteen inches long, six inches wide and only three or four inches deep. It looked like a small version of a bank safe deposit box. At one end were a set of bright copper connecters which had been plugged into data ports inside the nose cone.

Blake lifted the top off the box and looked at the chunky metal brick within. "Is this it? The storage drive or whatever it is?"

"It's some kind of solid-state drive, that's all I know about it. This was Jill's department. I don't think we should touch it. We'll bring the whole damned thing back with us."

Blake held it for a moment. Then he passed it to Jeffries. "You're the boss," he said. "And it looks like you've got what you came for. Now let's get back. Jill must be half-frozen by now."

Jeffries turned the module over in his hands. "It's so light," he said. "Can't weigh more than a couple of pounds." He bent to open his pack, stuffing the module inside. "Doesn't seem possible, does it? All that work for a thing this small?"

"Hurry up, let's go," yelled Blake over the wind. "We've still got to get down into the valley."

Behind him, Jeffries was still occupied with his pack. Blake clapped his hands together, trying to dispel the numbness. "Get a move on, Ed," he said, turning to face Jeffries. "We've got–"

He stopped, open-mouthed, as he saw the gun in Jeffries' ungloved hand. The muzzle came up slowly until it pointed directly at Blake's heart.

"Goodbye, Blake," Jeffries whispered. "You've been a big help. Don't think we're not grateful."

Then he fired, blowing Blake backwards, head over heels into the snow.

# CHAPTER SIXTEEN

Blake swam slowly back to consciousness, rising from dreams of cold and darkness into a whited-out world filled with the roaring of the wind. Someone was shaking him.

He moved, feeling white-hot pain course through his chest. He blinked, clearing his vision, and saw that he was sprawled face down on a slab of bare rock. He lay covered with snow, his arms and legs numb with cold. Images of Jeffries, the gun, and the shot flooded back into his brain, and he realized that he must be dying.

"Peter! Peter, wake up!" Someone shook him again. He glanced sideways and saw Winters' face only inches from his, her cheeks glistening with icy tears.

I'm still alive, he thought. "What happened?" he croaked.

She took his face between cold hands and began to cry. "Oh, Peter, I thought you were dead!" She sobbed, choking on the words.

Blake shook himself and rolled over, raising himself on his elbows. "What are you doing here?" He glanced around, blinking to clear his vision. "And where's Jeffries?"

"Ed's gone," she said simply. "Vanished. I waited and waited, but no one came. Then I must have fallen asleep. It was so cold, Peter."

She brushed clumsily at her eyes. "My hands are probably frozen by now. I can't feel anything in them at all. That's bad, isn't it?"

He nodded. His chest hurt. "Put your hands back into your parka," he said. "Turn your back to the wind; get in close to me." He took a painful breath and shook his head to clear it. "And keep talking. Tell me what happened."

She huddled close against him. "I don't know how long I was passed out. I woke up because part of the bivvy sack came undone. I remembered what you'd said about the wind chill factor, so I lit the stove and waited some more. I– I got into a panic, finally. I remembered the compass bearing for the nose cone, and so I came looking for you. I was afraid I'd gone too far – that I was lost. Then I saw you lying here. Peter, what in the name of God's happened?"

"Jeffries shot me," Blake said. "We extracted the data module, and the next thing I saw was his gun." He extended his hand. "Help me up, will you?"

Sitting up, braced against the wind, Blake carefully felt his chest, wincing at the touch of his fingers. Unbuttoning his parka, he explored the place where Jeffries had shot him. His frozen fingers came away sticky with blood.

He opened his shirt wider. There was a deep gash on the left side of his chest, and angry red marks around the area just below his heart. He stared up at Winters. "I don't understand this," he said. "He couldn't have missed. He shot me from less than ten feet away."

A second later he had the answer. Pulling on the rawhide thong, he drew out the heavy compass that he had kept under his shirt to prevent it from freezing up. The compass was nothing but a lump of twisted metal now, bent almost double by the force of the bullet, which had struck it nearly dead center.

Blake struggled to his feet, fighting the pain and nausea which washed over him. His watch read three o'clock.

With surprise, he realized that he had been lying in the snow for hours.

And where, he wondered, was Ed Jeffries? Looking around him, he saw that the storm had slackened somewhat; the wind was not as strong as before, and less snow was falling. But enough had already come down, he saw, to wipe out Jeffries' tracks.

Where had he gone? He turned to Winters. "You didn't see Jeffries? He should have come right by where you were."

She shook her head. "The storm was so bad that I couldn't see more than a few feet. And I was asleep for most of the time. He could have walked straight past me."

"But he didn't stop and get you."

She shook her head. "No, he didn't. Where do you think he is?"

"He must have gone back to the camp," Blake said. "There's food there, and equipment. He'll have gone there before starting down into the valley."

She looked at him, her hands shoved deep in her parka. "You mean he's left us here to die?"

Blake agreed. "It looks that way, doesn't it?"

He beat his arms together to restore feeling in them, willing his brain to work. Jeffries was gone, and with him the emergency food and water. All Blake had been carrying, he remembered, was the first aid kit, the signal flares, some parachute cord and the extra bottle of stove fuel. He knelt and checked the contents of his rucksack. It was all still there.

He glanced up at her. "Do you still have the stove?"

"No," she said miserably. "I left it behind, like a fool. I brought the bivvy sack, though. It's folded up in my pack."

"Good," said Blake. "We're going to need it."

He was thinking fast now, trying to calculate his next moves carefully. They would need proper shelter soon, and food and water. He had eaten nothing since the morning, and now he could feel hunger building inside him, a counterpoint to the pain in his ribs. It would be dark in a few hours, and with darkness the temperature would drop still further. And if, as he suspected, they were in the eye of the storm now, the snow and wind would return, stronger than before.

He fought down his rising panic as he listened to the icy wind. If they did not do something soon, both of them would die. Without shelter, their bodies would work overtime to produce life-sustaining heat. Without food, the body's heat output could not be sustained, and so their organs would begin to fail, one by one.

It would take time, he knew, but the process of dying had already begun for both of them. Their bodies were withdrawing heat from the extremities, shutting them down in an effort to protect the brain and the vital organs in thorax. Soon they would fall unconscious, slipping into a coma from which they would never awaken.

Winters was already showing visible signs of hypothermia; she trembled uncontrollably, her lips pinched tight and her eyes half-closed. And inside Blake's head, a tiny voice had begun to whisper, telling him to lie down, rest, close his eyes. Just for a little while. Just for a moment.

She gripped his shoulder. "Are we going to die?"

He wrapped her in his arms, feeling the tears begin on her frozen cheeks. "Your compass. Have you still got your compass?"

She nodded.

"Then we're not going to die. Not yet. Come on."

He turned her gently. Hanging on to each other, they began to stumble back down the ridge, towards the overhang. Beyond the overhang lay the camp, and their last remaining chance of survival.

# CHAPTER SEVENTEEN

They lay huddled together, wedged into the bivvy sack, hidden in the rocks at the base of the overhang. The camp lay further down the slope, just visible through the clearing mist.

Winters' face was an ivory mask, her breathing was weak and shallow. She was exhausted, Blake knew, and slipping fast into unconsciousness. He held her hands clamped firmly under his armpits, trying to restore circulation to her frozen fingers. He squeezed her tightly, trying to will his own remaining warmth into her.

Six o'clock had come and gone now, and darkness was falling. The storm had slackened somewhat; the clouds were higher now, and the snow had temporarily stopped. In the waning light, Blake could make out the outlines of the two tents in the distance, one of them illuminated from inside by the soft yellow glow of a lantern.

The last three hours have been a waking nightmare, he thought, shivering as he drew Winters closer. They had stumbled along the summit ridge for an eternity, never able to see more than a few feet in any direction. Twice, Blake had nearly plunged off the ridge.

Dragging the nearly unconscious woman, he had slowly made his way back to the overhang above their camp. Blake had managed to find the piton anchors, still solid in the rock, but the ropes were gone; Jeffries had pulled them through the carabiners after he had descended. Blake gave a low moan of despair. They were trapped at the top of the cliff. As darkness fell, so once again would the temperature, and he knew they would not survive the night on the exposed ridge.

Then he had remembered the nylon parachute cord in his pack. It was barely long enough, and it had a breaking strength of only five hundred pounds, but it would have to do. With trembling fingers, he undid the coil. *It would have to do.*

The nylon cord had held, and now they were safe. They were past the overhang, and relatively secure – for the moment – on the sloping ground of the summit ridge. Blake peered again at the lantern light coming from the tent. He would have to make his move now, while they still lay in the eye of the storm. The weather would turn again, he knew, in less than an hour or so. He had to find food and shelter before then. Or die.

Time to move. He forced the last remaining bits of chocolate into his mouth and got painfully to his knees. He wrapped the bivvy sack tightly around Winters, banking snow against the sides for greater insulation. She stirred, looking up at him with blank eyes.

"Where are you going, Peter?" she whispered, her teeth chattering.

He bent to her ear. "Jeffries is still in the tent," he said softly. "I'm going over to deal with him. The storm will start again soon, and we've got to get under cover." He touched her cheek. "Hang on for just a while longer."

She bit her lip. "Peter, don't do it. He's got a gun – he'll kill you."

Blake shook his head. "He had his chance to kill me, and he failed," he said. "It's my turn now."

He rose and eased his pack straps over his shoulders, glancing up at the night sky. No moon – that would help. He had no idea what he was going to do when he got to the camp, but darkness would be an advantage for whatever was about to happen. Staggering a little, he began to make his way down the ridge, through the snow to the tents.

He'd think of something when the time came, he told himself. He'd have to.

* * *

He had crawled to within twenty feet of the lighted tent when he found the body of Ed Jeffries, half buried in the snow.

Blake knew what it was as soon as he brushed against it. Now he lay still, his heart thudding, while he inspected the corpse. Jeffries was lying face down in the snow, angled away from the tent. He could see gaping wounds in Jeffries' back where three bullets had torn into him from behind. His bloody footprints, still faintly visible, were wide, as if he had been running. All around, the snow was dark with frozen blood.

Taking off his gloves, he felt the body. Stone cold, and stiff with rigor mortis. Jeffries had been lying there for several hours, possibly longer. Blake glanced nervously at the lighted tent, and just then, on a gust of wind, he heard the voices.

There they were again. Two voices, talking inside the tent. They drifted past him on the wind, no words distinguishable. He wormed his way closer, crawling another few feet on knees and elbows, biting his lips against the cold. He could feel his ribs grinding painfully as he inched across the snow.

Now he could see shadows on the tent wall, backlit by the lantern. Two men, sitting down, talking to each other in animated voices. From time to time, one of them would laugh.

Something's very wrong, he thought. Whoever was inside the tent had shot Jeffries. But the only person who should be in the tent right now was Ray Corley. And Ray should be flat on his back, not sitting up and laughing.

Then who are these people? There's only one possible answer, Blake thought. The two men they had seen on the grasslands earlier that morning. The two who had carried the automatic rifles strapped to their packs.

They had managed to scale the rock wall before the storm hit. And somehow, through incredibly good luck, they had stumbled on the camp, hidden in the mist. They had been waiting for Jeffries when he'd returned from the summit, and they had killed him. And then they must have taken the data module.

Crawling back to where Jeffries lay, Blake searched the corpse thoroughly. No module, and no gun.

Blake was trapped here, with no weapon, while his hunters sat, warm and safe, not ten yards away.

There was movement inside the tent, and the flap suddenly opened. Blake dropped flat onto the snow and slid crabwise back into the darkness as a figure emerged from the tent and stood up.

"*Sheiße, es ist verdammt kalt hier draußen!*"

An answering laugh came from within the tent. German, Blake thought. They were Germans.

The man who had come outside turned and muttered something to his companion inside. In the light spilling through the open flap, Blake could see him clearly. Tall and with a thick moustache, he wore a parka with a fur-lined hood. In one hand he carried an automatic rifle; in the other, a lighted cigarette. The man paused, hefted the rifle, and began to walk slowly across the snow, straight toward where Blake lay.

Heart thudding, Blake lay still, watching as the man approached to within ten feet of him. His rifle, held negligently at his side, pointed straight at his head. The man stopped in front of Jeffries' body, planted his feet wide apart, and flicked his cigarette away. It hissed into the snow not three feet from Blake's face.

Night-blindness, he thought. He can't see me yet. But he will, if he stays out here long enough.

A voice from inside the tent called out a question, and the man in front of him gave a short, harsh reply.

The man fumbled with the front of his trousers for a moment. Then, still holding his weapon in one hand, he began to urinate on Jeffries' body. The sharp odor of ammonia filled Blake's nostrils, and he held himself rigidly, suppressing the strong urge to retch. After a long moment, the man finished. He took one last quick glance at his surroundings, muttered something to himself, and stumped back toward the tent.

Blake slowly let his breath out and edged forward again. Inside the tent, the two men seemed to be having an argument. First one voice was raised, then the other. Blake lay shivering in the snow and listened. After several more stormy exchanges, the issue had apparently been decided. The mustached man emerged once more from the tent, hauling a large rucksack with him. He positioned this in front of the tent and sat down heavily on it, cradling his rifle across his knees. He lit a cigarette, muttering darkly to himself. Behind him, the light inside the tent went out.

They're keeping watch, thought Blake. They know Jeffries wasn't alone, and they're taking no chances. He stole a glance at his watch. Seven o'clock now. The storm would begin again at any time, he reminded himself. They could not survive a night in the open.

He had to get himself and Winters into the tent, into the warmth and the shelter. And quickly. He began to inch backwards through the snow, burrowing deeper, watching the German with hungry, slitted eyes. Already it seemed as if the wind had picked up again.

He had very little time to think of something.

# CHAPTER EIGHTEEN

Everything was ready now. Only the mechanics remained. Blake lay in the snow, watching the German guard and trying hard to control the chattering of his teeth.

The night had turned sharp and cold. The wind was stronger now, and snow had started to fall again. Good, thought Blake. The wind and snow would help to cover any noise he might make.

The guard huddled motionless on his perch, gun across his knees. He chain-smoked cigarettes, his furry hood pulled up tight and close against the cold. From time to time, he stamped his feet to warm them.

He had been sitting there for nearly half an hour, and in that time, Blake had worked out exactly how he was going to kill him.

Only one thing matters now, Blake thought. The German must stay where he is for another ten minutes. After that, he can move, can go inside the tent. The sooner the better, in fact. Before I turn to ice.

But first, ten minutes to make the necessary preparations. Flexing his cramped muscles to keep the circulation going, Blake began his work.

Moving very slowly, he slid his rucksack off his shoulders and quietly opened the flap, keeping himself well hidden. He would have only one chance to kill them, he knew. The Germans were armed, alert and highly professional. They must be in top physical condition,

Blake thought, to have scaled the rock wall so quickly. And God alone knows how they've managed to find our camp in the thick mist.

He stood no chance at all against them at close quarters, he thought as his bare hand explored the interior of the rucksack. He had no doubt that they would kill him if they discovered him. They would kill him and Winters both, and throw their bodies over the side into a clump of brush or down a wide rock crevice. Who would ever search for them here? And if they did search, how would they ever find them?

Blake needed two things from his pack, and both of them, he remembered, would be at the bottom. Inch by inch, he worked his hand down inside, careful not to let the pieces of climbing hardware clink together. Finally, he felt the smooth cold metal of the bottle of stove fuel. Gripping it tightly, he withdrew it from the pack and set it carefully on the snow beside him.

One item down. One to go.

Reaching into the pack again, he groped blindly at the bottom. He was searching for something small and flat, and as the seconds ticked by, he began to wonder if he had brought it after all. Then, to his immense relief, his fingers closed around the small metal box, and a moment later, he drew out the emergency flares.

Now he was ready. But first, he had to get closer.

* * *

Several minutes later, Blake was in position, five yards away from the entrance to the tent. He lay off to one side, away from the German's immediate field of vision. Keeping down, he reached behind him and drew the fuel bottle forward. Then he pried open the box of flares.

The flare launcher was a simple device: an eight-inch metal tube with a firing trigger at one end. The end of the tube contained a powerful spring, actuated by the trigger. There were six flares in the box – short, metal tubes the size of a fat fountain pen and filled with colored phosphorus. There were, Blake remembered, two green flares, two red flares, and two white flares.

He picked one out at random in the dark. It doesn't matter in the least what color it was, he thought. Just as long as it fires when the time comes.

Firing, too, was simple. The flare had to be inserted, percussion cap down, into the barrel of the firing tube. Then the flare had to be pushed all the way down against the spring, compressing it and cocking the small firing pin in the base of the launcher tube. When the trigger stud was pressed, the pin would strike the flare, exploding the percussion cap and igniting the phosphorus, while at the same time the strong spring shot the flare high into the sky.

The flares are supposed to go up at least three hundred feet, thought Blake, but that doesn't matter, either. This flare won't be going up. It won't be going very far at all, in fact.

The German stirred. He stood up, slapping snow from his boots, and reached inside the pocket of his parka for another cigarette. Taking advantage of the noise and the movement, Blake quickly found the recessed dimple on the flare and inserted it into the barrel of the launcher. There was a soft click as he pushed the flare down against the spring.

Holding the flare in one hand, he reached behind him with the other and grasped the fuel bottle. He felt for the pressure cap at the top. It would open with a flick of the wrist, one-handed. The bottle held two liters, and it was nearly full.

The German was still standing, cigarette in his mouth, fumbling for the lighter. He snapped it half a dozen times, with no success. Cursing, the man bent to the tent, lifted the flap, and crawled back inside.

Blake moved quickly. In a matter of seconds, the man would be coming out again. Coming up into a crouching position, he faced the tent and popped the cap from the fuel bottle. Rising, he hobbled awkwardly to within ten feet of the open tent flap. Inside, he could hear the two men talking.

He threw the opened fuel bottle underhand, like a softball, into the tent.

Silvery fuel spilled from the bottle's mouth as it turned end over end, landing just inside the tent flap. From inside, there was a muffled exclamation. Blake brought the flare launcher up and fired it directly into the tent.

The next few seconds were nightmarish. There was a sharp snap and a whoosh as the flare, already burning, shot from the tube. It tore into the tent with a loud hissing noise, lighting up the entire area, turning the campsite into the high noon of an atomic explosion.

Blake dropped to the snow as the fuel in the bottle exploded with tremendous force, blowing the tent off the ground. The concussion slapped him as a giant fireball leaped twenty feet into the air. He could hear the whine of metal pieces flying past his head.

It was a scene from hell. Getting to his feet, Blake saw that the explosion had blown apart the sides of the tent. The synthetic material had ignited instantly, and was now blazing fiercely. The fuel bottle contained a liquid more volatile than gasoline; it had needed only the smallest spark to ignite. Confined by its metal bottle, it had exploded like an incendiary bomb.

The walls of the tent were nearly burned away now. Inside, Blake could see two flame-wreathed figures beating helplessly at themselves, trying to extinguish the blaze. As if from a great distance, he could hear screams, and then he realized that he had been partially deafened by the explosion.

The two fiery creatures jerked and capered in the flame light like demented marionettes. Blake dropped to the ground again as a burst of automatic fire erupted from the rifle that one of the men still clutched. The shots were wild, going in all directions as the man's seared muscles contracted in the heat of the fire. There were two more sporadic bursts, and then silence.

In a moment, it was over. Their screams died away and the two huddled, blackened bodies stopped twitching. Pieces of the tent continued to flicker and burn, lighting up Blake's face as he gazed, horror-struck, at what he had done.

He stood quietly in the snow, watching as the fires guttered down to glowing embers. Then he remembered the second tent, five yards away in the snow. It was still intact. Crossing to it, he ripped open the flap and shone his torch inside. Ray Corley lay just as they had left him hours ago, still wrapped in sleeping bags. Behind him, their food and equipment lay piled, and on top of that, the data module that Jeffries had taken from the nose cone.

He reached out to shake Corley awake. His hand touched a body that was as cold as ice, as lifeless as the snow itself. He shone his light on the dead man's face, its features calm and composed. He must have expired hours ago, Blake thought.

Gasping from the effort, he dragged Corley's body outside and laid it in the snow next to the two Germans. Then, without warning, the tension of the past hours broke; Blake vomited feebly into the snow, dropping to his knees as the spasm took control of him. He remained on all fours until the sickness and the trembling receded.

He had to get Winters, he remembered. Getting to his feet, he removed the heavy gloves from Corley's hands. Snapping on his light, he began to stagger back up along the ridge to where he had left Winters, hoping that it was not too late. That she, at least, was still alive.

# CHAPTER NINETEEN

The storm lasted all night, finally clearing in the hours just after dawn. Jill Winters came awake at noon.

Blake made soup and tea for her, holding her upright while she took small sips, watching the color come back gradually into her face. Eventually she focused on him, brushed hair out of her eyes, and frowned. "Where are we? Where are the others?"

Blake told her the whole story. He left nothing out. As he spoke, her eyes widened and her lips began to tremble.

"Oh, God," she said in an unsteady voice. "All dead?"

He folded his arms around her, patting her the way one would a child. "All dead. Outside."

She took a deep breath. "Show me."

He helped her into her parka and together they crawled out of the tent and into the clear, cold air. Under the fresh snow, the bodies and the blasted tent were still clearly visible. Winters stood for a moment gazing at the wreckage. Then she put her hands to her face and began to cry, her shoulders moving convulsively.

Blake led her back inside and made more tea. She drank it in silence, and then she said, "It's horrible, isn't it? Did you know the fuel was going to explode like that?"

"I hoped it might," he replied. "I was counting on it, in fact."

"But – dying that way. Up here, away from everything. Burned alive like that. My God."

He took her arm. "There wasn't any other way, Jill. They'd already killed Jeffries, and they were going to kill us, too." He pointed to the data module behind her. "That's what they were after. Our lives didn't count."

She glared back at him angrily. "I don't care. It's still horrible."

He touched her cheek gently with a fingertip. "Jill." He spoke softly. "You and I are alive right now because they're dead. It's as simple as that."

Her expression clouded. "You've changed, Peter," she said after a moment. "There's something different about you now. You wouldn't have said that a few days ago."

Blake shrugged. "Changed? Maybe. But the rules of the game have changed, too. And this time, I'm playing to win." He took her face in his hands. "We're going to survive, Jill. You and I are going to make it, no matter what. No more running."

She shivered and came back into his arms. "What are we going to do now, Peter?" Her voice came as if from far away.

He pulled the sleeping bag around her and took away the mug of tea. "Get some rest for now," he said. "How are your fingers? Can you feel anything?"

"A little. Not much."

"You'll have to see a doctor soon, I think. But first we have to get out of here. The storm's over. Tomorrow, we'll start walking back to the airstrip at Wambip."

"And after that?"

He shook his head. "We'll take care of everything when the time comes. Now go back to sleep. I've got a few things to do."

* * *

At first, the thought of touching their bodies made him want to throw up again. The first German was the hardest. Blake's flesh shrank as he bent and picked up one end of the charred lump of meat that had once been a living person. The second German was next, then Corley.

By the time Blake came to Jeffries, he could have done a dozen more.

He pushed them one by one over the side of the ridge. They would fall three hundred feet at least, he estimated, before they disappeared into the thick brush lining the valley's sides. With luck, no one would ever discover their bodies.

He disposed of the Germans' equipment in the same way, keeping back a few items for later inspection. One of these was a heavy leather pouch hidden underneath the Germans' climbing hardware, untouched by fire. Pulling it out, he opened it. Inside was Jeffries' gun, and something else, in a sturdy envelope. Slitting it open, Blake stared open-mouthed at the thick stack of banknotes. There were five-hundred-euro notes, in four bands of one hundred each. Two hundred thousand euros, he thought. For what? And for whom?

He stood, balancing the gun and the money in his hands, frowning. Then he stuffed them both inside the pockets of his parka and turned back to the tent.

\* \* \*

Later in the afternoon, Winters woke again to find Blake hunched over the radio equipment, cursing softly to himself.

"What are you doing?" she said sleepily.

"Trying to figure something out," he replied, snapping on the radio beacon. The needle on the battery indicator flickered once, and then lay still. Blake set the beacon aside. He picked up the broken transceiver and started to remove the back.

Winters came fully awake now, propping herself up on one elbow. "Peter, what are you doing?"

Blake pulled the battery out of the transceiver. "I was wondering," he said slowly, "how the Germans managed to find our camp yesterday." He disconnected the battery terminals as he spoke. "We were completely socked in, remember? Finding our camp in that weather would have been a miracle." He turned to look at her. "I don't think it happened by accident."

"What are you talking about?"

"Give me a second."

Quickly, he connected the transceiver's battery to the radio beacon. This time, the indicator needle swung over hard, indicating a full battery charge.

"Look at that," he said quietly. "The beacon's battery is dead, but the transceiver's isn't. We haven't used either of them. We couldn't use the transceiver because it was sabotaged; and we never needed to use the beacon." He picked up the grey metal box. "But somebody used the beacon – its battery is dead. Absolutely flat. Somebody turned the beacon on, and it led the Germans straight to us." He pulled out the remains of the receiver that he had found in the Germans' equipment. "Somebody up here turned on the signal, and the Germans picked it up on this. It led them straight to us."

Winters' face was pinched. "One of us?"

Blake nodded. "I think it was Ray Corley."

"Ray? No, Ray wouldn't–"

"It had to be him. The rest of us were on the mountain. Corley knew they were behind us; he'd probably been in contact with them earlier. I think he sabotaged the radio before we ever began to climb the rock wall to the ridge. Then we left him here, and that's when he turned the signal on for them."

She was staring at him, open-mouthed. "Then Ed–"

"Jeffries came back to camp intending to kill Corley and get away into the valley on his own. He'd already shot me and left you to die. It would have been easy for him to get down the ridge alone, and he knew how to rig a rappel. He was in good condition, and he was alone," Blake said. "He'd have made it, I think."

He started to repack the radio. "At first, I thought it must have been Jeffries who alerted the Germans. He'd tried to kill me, after all. But there are a couple of things that don't make sense."

"Such as?"

"It was Jeffries who fell into the river on that first day, remember? He was convinced that someone had pulled on the rope. I think he was right. Later, Jeffries was the one who kept us going, once we'd spotted the Germans. He was desperate to get away from them. And then there's the fact that the Germans killed Jeffries in the end, but not Corley."

"So it had to be Ray," she said slowly.

"Yes. Jeffries had his own double-cross planned, of course: killing me, leaving you, and getting off the mountain alone. He was desperate to get his hands on the data module – we all know that. I don't know... maybe he and Ray were in it together, and something went wrong at the end. Maybe both of them were working for the Germans." He looked at Winters. "It's not worth trying to figure it out. The important thing is that they're dead, and we're alive."

"But why, Peter? What would either of them gain from helping the Germans? That's what doesn't make sense."

Blake gave her a thin smile as he took one of the packets of banknotes from his parka. "For the money," he said. "They had two hundred thousand euros, Jill. We all know that the data in the module was worth a lot. We know that Corley didn't trust Amos Sanford. Maybe Ed Jeffries didn't either. The Germans just got in first with a better offer. That's what it looks like to me."

He moved close and put his arm around her. "It's going to be all right, Jill. We're alive. We've got the data module and the money. It's over. We're safe now."

She put her cheek against his, gently, and held him close. "Are we?" she murmured. "I wonder."

# CHAPTER TWENTY

In the afternoon of the next day, they staggered out of the forest into a clearing, dropped their packs, and sank to the ground, exhausted. Blake recognized the place as the lookout point from which they had seen the second aircraft landing at Wambip. What had their guide called it? 'The place where people die'.

Well, we're not dead yet, thought Blake. Not by a long shot. Not yet. He fumbled more aspirin out of his pack and ate two, swallowing them without water. His head ached constantly now, and his body felt like it was burning up. Infection had set in, and unless they could get to medical help soon, it might kill him.

Winters was not much better. Although feeling had come back to her frozen hands, the skin looked blackened and ugly. She was emotionally and physically used up; he had been carrying her most of the way through the rainforest. Getting down the rock wall had been the easiest part, in a way. Blake had used their remaining climbing hardware to rig a series of rappels down the sheer face. By strapping Winters to his back with a sling and rigging a friction brake on the rope, he had managed to bring them both down without incident. They had abandoned their ropes and other equipment on the *kunai* plateau, taking only essential food and the first aid kit for the trip down through the rainforest to the village.

And the data module, the money and the gun, of course.

Blake lay back and stared at the clouds. The air was warm and humid, and he felt relaxed and safe. It's hard to believe, he thought lazily, that only a few thousand feet above exists a land of snow and ice. And death.

But that world exists far away from here, he thought, as he turned over to look at Winters. A world that they would never visit again. She had fallen asleep, her head propped awkwardly against her pack. He adjusted her position and lay back down beside her. So tired, he thought. We'll just rest here for an hour. Just for a bit. We can still make it to the village by nightfall.

Just rest a bit. So tired.

\* \* \*

Blake snapped awake, stirred by sharp pains in his chest. Opening his eyes, he saw the barrel of an ancient Enfield rifle prodding his cracked ribs. His gaze followed the rifle upward to the short brown man dressed in camouflage fatigues holding it. On his shoulders were the insignia of the Indonesian Army. His expression was tense as he prodded Blake again with the gun barrel.

"*Bangun! Bangunlah!*"

Blake shook his head. "What the hell–"

The gun barrel swung up, catching him painfully on the cheek.

"*Sekarang!*"

The man's voice was rough with tension and anger. Behind the anger, the man was also very frightened, Blake saw. He grabbed Blake by the collar of his parka and hauled him to his feet.

Blake steadied himself, pulled away and looked around. Another soldier with a rifle was guarding Winters, who still slept, unmindful of the danger. There appeared to be no one else in the clearing. They're part of an Indonesian border patrol, thought Blake, his pulse beginning to race.

He should have anticipated this. They should have waited until they were hidden in the forest before resting.

He raised his hands slowly. The soldier took a cautious step backward, jerking up the gun barrel, his eyes dark and watchful.

"*Siapa namamu?*"

"I don't understand you," Blake said slowly and quietly. "Do you speak English?"

"*Apa?*"

"English. Do you speak English?"

"*Inggris? Tidak!*"

He motioned Blake forward with the rifle. His companion jerked Winters awake roughly, ignoring her cry of alarm. Blake eyed his pack, on the ground in front of him, containing Jeffries' gun. Forget it, he told himself. You'd be shot dead in seconds.

Blake's guardian noted his glance. Bending, he picked up the pack and pointed down the trail.

"*Ayo, pergi!*"

The motion of his rifle left no doubt as to the meaning of the command. They were to follow him back to the government patrol post.

"Peter?" Winters spoke as they entered the forest. He swung to look at her. "Peter, can't we do something? They're taking us in the wrong direction!"

He shook his head. "Do as they say," he murmured. "We don't have any choice right now. I don't think they understand English, so maybe we can—"

The soldier following Blake gave a soft grunt, and a moan. Blake turned to see the tip of a black palm spear protruding from the front of his uniform, blood already spilling from the soldier's open mouth. As he watched, the man folded up and fell to the ground.

The second soldier, seeing this, gave a short shriek of exclamation, turned, and ran into the jungle, dropping his gun in the process. A moment later there was a high scream from within the bushes, followed by silence.

Blake had thrown himself flat on the ground, pulling Winters down beside him.

"What in—"

"Sssh," he whispered, putting his hand over her mouth. The forest around them stayed quiet for a long moment, and then, three figures stepped out onto the path. One of them was Imea, their guide from Wambip village.

Blake sat up. "Imea! Why—"

"Don't speak." Imea spoke softly, holding up a hand. "There may be others close to us." After a moment, he turned and murmured quietly to his companions. They melted away into the forest, taking the dead soldier with them.

When they had disappeared, Imea turned to Blake. "Do you have cigarettes?"

Blake scrabbled in his pack and found the remains of a tattered packet that had once belonged to Winters. He passed them over. Imea lit one, inhaled appreciatively, and squatted down on his haunches.

"They kill us because they want to frighten us, to show us how powerful they are," he said quietly after a moment. "They do not like us hunting here; they say it is their land." He spat. "But this was our land long before they came here, and it is still our land. Their guns and uniforms make no difference."

He puffed deeply on his cigarette. "So they kill us when they catch us, and we kill them when we catch them." He grinned suddenly, showing large white teeth. "We are better at it than they are. Most of them are very afraid to be here. They are afraid of the forest." He gestured out into the dense foliage. "We will take their guns and hide the bodies where no one will ever see."

He stood up. "Now we must go. Before more soldiers come. You will come back with us to the village."

"Thank you for saving us," Blake said.

Imea shrugged. "It was necessary. If they had taken you, there would have been trouble. They would come to

149

the village and search; they pay no attention to the border, just like us. They always hit the old men and insult our women when they come to the village. This way, things are better. More simple, I think. Come on."

As Blake shouldered his pack, Imea said quietly, "There is only you and the woman. And you are both hurt. Where are the others?"

Blake remained silent.

Imea searched his eyes carefully. "Something bad has happened," he said. "I will not ask you now, but the elders will ask you. And you must tell them."

He turned and began to walk down the trail to the village.

# CHAPTER TWENTY-ONE

A small child playing in the mud at the edge of the village was the first to notice them as they emerged from the trees. The screams quickly brought his mother, whose excited shouts summoned others. Within seconds, a crowd of thirty people stood staring at them and whispering.

Imea came up to stand beside Blake. "Come," he said. "My father's hut. This way."

The hut was a one-roomed shack on stilts, with woven pit-pit walls and a thatched roof. They climbed the short set of stairs to a wide veranda and entered the single room behind it. Inside was a large wooden bed and a crude table, together with several chairs. Two kerosene lamps stood on the table. Over in the corner, beside the bed, was a low wooden trunk, open to reveal folded clothes and blankets.

"You can rest here," Imea said. "The elders will come tonight."

"What day is it?" said Blake.

Imea looked at him in surprise. "Saturday, of course. Why?"

"Then the plane comes tomorrow."

"Yes," he said. "The plane comes. If there is good weather." He reached for Blake's pack. "Let me hang this up for you."

Blake pushed his hand away. "I'll manage, thanks."

Imea looked at him curiously. "As you wish."

* * *

That evening, Blake washed himself from a bucket of warm water on the back veranda, using a tin can for a dipper and glorying in the luxury of it. When he had finished, he helped Winters wash. Her body was burning with fever, and he dosed her with aspirin before dressing his own wounds.

He had lifted her to the large bed and was making her comfortable when there was a rapping on the door. Blake opened the door to find Imea in the darkness, looking solemn. Behind him, on the ground below the veranda, stood a small crowd of men. In the forefront was the headman in his red cap.

"They are very frightened," Imea began without preamble. "They see that you are both hurt, and they do not see your friends. They say that we will have to tell the *kiap* – the government officer – in Telefomin. The police will come, and there will be much trouble. The police will say that we have killed your friends, and then we will all go to prison. That is what they say."

He paused.

"Now they want to talk to you. You must tell them the truth about what has happened." He lowered his voice. "There is no need to mention the Indonesian soldiers. That will only make them more afraid."

Blake looked out again at the assembled group. All of them wore grim, worried expressions. Winters edged out slowly onto the veranda.

"What's happening, Peter?" she whispered. "Are they going to hurt us?"

"I don't think so," he replied in a low voice. "They just want to find out what happened. Go inside and get the gun from my pack. Keep it out of sight, but somewhere you can lay hands on it in a hurry. I'll deal with them."

She nodded and went back inside.

"Tell the men to come inside," Blake said to Imea. "I'll need you to translate."

A dozen old men arranged themselves on the floor of the hut. Imea hung the kerosene lamps from the rafters, their dim light casting deep shadows into the corners of the small room. Outside, the rest of the village waited in the darkness, talking quietly among themselves.

The headman spoke first.

"He asks about your friends," said Imea. "He is worried for the village. He says the *kiap* will blame our people; will say we killed those men for their money. It will be bad, and we will all be sent to prison. The headman says that he will go to prison, too, for he has taken some of the white man's money. Now he wants to know where your friends are."

Blake licked his cracked lips. He glanced at Winters and saw her imperceptible nod. Good, he thought; she has the gun ready. We'll never be able to shoot our way out of here, but we might negotiate a stand-off, if things get nasty.

"My friends are dead," he began quietly.

There was an audible intake of breath from the assembled elders as Imea translated.

"There was an accident. We were climbing the rock wall, above the *kunai* plateau. The rope broke, and they fell. Both died, instantly."

"And when did this happen?" the old man asked.

"The day after the guides left us," Blake replied. "We tried to climb the rock wall, and they fell. That's how it happened."

The old man counted on his fingers. "That was many days ago. Why did you wait so long to return?"

Blake pointed at Winters. "The woman was also injured and could not travel. Then the storm came." He indicated his own injuries. "We are both sick and hurt. We need to go to Mount Hagen and then to Port Moresby, to the hospital there."

As Imea translated, there was a swelling murmur of comment from the elders. Then the headman asked the question Blake had been waiting for.

"And the other two men. Where are they?"

Blake kept his eyes steady on Imea. "What other men is he talking about?"

Imea looked surprised. "You remember – the ones who came in the airplane on the day after you arrived. We both saw them from the clearing on the ridge, when they landed." He paused. "The whole village is talking about them. One was tall; the other had a moustache. They wanted no carriers, they let no one near their packs. They went along the same trail that you took. When we met them on our way back to the village, they asked us about you. No one has seen them since. Where are they?"

Everyone was looking at Blake, waiting for his answer. "We did not see them," he said at last, keeping his voice even. "We don't know who they were. Perhaps they took the wrong trail, and got lost in the forest. It is easy to do, without guides."

An excited babble broke out amongst the men. The headman roared for silence. When calm had been restored, he spoke quietly to Imea.

Imea turned to Blake. "He is afraid for the village. He says such a thing has never happened before. He wants to keep you here until the police come. The *balus* – the plane – will come tomorrow. They can radio Telefomin."

Blake shook his head. "We're sick and injured," he repeated. "We have to go to Mount Hagen on the plane tomorrow morning. We'll explain everything to the police there. But we have to leave tomorrow."

A long argument began among the elders. When it was over, Imea's face was glistening with sweat. He turned to Blake.

"They say no," he said. "You must stay here. They will send a message with the pilot tomorrow, but you must stay here."

His voice dropped. "I think you should do what they say. They are very frightened. Some of them say that you have killed those other men. Some of them say... they say that we should kill you now and hide your bodies in the forest. Then no one will ever know. But the headman does not agree – he wants to give you to the police."

His eyes pleaded silently with Blake. "You must tell them that you will stay and wait for the police. Do not argue or make trouble. If you do, there will be violence. They are ready to kill you, believe me."

Blake stared at him for a long moment. "Very well," he said. "We will stay."

"Good." Imea spoke with visible relief. "I will sleep outside tonight and keep you safe."

The meeting was over. The old men shouldered their axes and shuffled out the door and into the night, fear and anger showing plainly on their faces. We're lepers, thought Blake, bringers of calamity. They're very frightened, and about two steps away from violence. We'll have to be very careful. Very careful indeed.

When they had gone, Imea took up a position on the veranda outside their room. Below, small groups of villagers stood in the darkness and watched the hut, smoking and talking in low tones. All of them, Blake saw, were armed with either axes or knives.

He turned from the window and looked at Winters. "Well, we're prisoners," he said.

Her face was pale in the dim light of the lantern. "And the police aren't going to help us, are they? Peter, we've got to get out of here."

"We will," said Blake. He picked up Jeffries' gun. "We'll shoot our way out if we have to." He released the magazine and inspected the contents. Four brass shells gleamed dully in the lantern light. "Not a lot of firepower, but it gives us a bit of an edge. I just wish I'd brought one of the weapons the Germans had."

Winters shivered. "Don't talk about the Germans," she said quietly. "And when we get back to Mount Hagen? What then?"

Blake glanced out the window. "One step at a time," he said. "Let's get out of here first." He stretched. "We need some sleep. Tomorrow's going to be a tough day."

They fell asleep in the wide wooden bed, overcome by fever and exhaustion. In sleep, Blake held Winters' hand lightly in one of his own. In the other, he clutched the gun.

# CHAPTER TWENTY-TWO

Imea heard it first. He cocked his head, listening. "Plane's coming now," he said. "It's early."

A moment later, Blake could hear it too; a faint drone above the murmuring of the crowd, still waiting outside the hut in the dawn light. "Here we go," he said to Winters. "Get your boots on and be ready to move."

Blake raised his binoculars and scanned the sky, locating the aircraft as it drifted up the valley toward the village, wings wobbling slightly in the early-morning thermals. He came back inside and picked up the gun.

"It's an Islander, but a different one from before," he said. "A red and white one this time."

Winters looked at him, then at the gun. "What are you going to do, Peter?"

"Get us on the damned plane," he replied, snapping off the safety. "Follow me, and keep your head down."

They emerged onto the veranda and were greeted by a low roar of anger as the villagers spotted the gun in Blake's hand. Keeping it high and visible, he fired one shot into the air. Anger turned to terror as the people scattered, running wildly for cover among the huts. Imea's eyes were wide with fright as he watched Blake.

Blake took a step forward and grasped Imea's arm, turning him around and pushing him forward. He placed the gun gently in the small of his back. "Let's go," said Blake. "I'm sorry to do this, but I will shoot you if I have to. We're getting on that plane. You need to tell your friends here not to try and stop us!"

Imea's voice rang out clearly as they descended the steps, and the villagers backed away from them as if they'd suddenly become contagious. There was total silence in the village, broken only by the sound of the approaching plane.

They began to walk between the huts toward the airstrip. Blake pushed Imea in front of him, sweeping his eyes from side to side. From low doorways, silent faces watched them pass. At the edge of his vision, Blake could see people closing in behind them, keeping a safe distance. From somewhere, a child began to cry.

They stopped at the edge of the grass airstrip. Thirty feet away, the villagers also stopped and stood in a tight knot, watching. The Islander touched down at the end of the runway and gunned its motors, props flashing in the morning sunlight as it climbed the slight upgrade to where they stood. Blake waved his arm, and received an answering wave from the pilot.

The plane reached the end of the runway and swung around, fifty feet away. The engines revved one last time, and then dropped back to idle.

Blake turned to Winters. "Get ready to run for it." Releasing Imea, he tossed the gun to her. "Put this inside your parka, and let's go. I'll take the rucksack."

Together, they began to run toward the plane.

A roar erupted from behind them as the villagers started in pursuit. An axe whizzed into the ground beside Blake, and he heard Winters' gasp of fright.

"Keep going!" he shouted, dragging her still faster toward the waiting plane.

The crowd raced after the two fleeing figures, steadily closing the gap. Up ahead, the pilot had grasped the situation, and Blake saw the cockpit door swing open as the motors revved up in preparation for a quick takeoff.

They reached the plane not ten seconds ahead of the nearest villager. Heaving Winters and the rucksack aboard,

Blake used the open door as a shield against the rain of stones, sticks and axes which began to pelt the Islander with deadly accuracy.

"Take off, for Christ's sake!" he shouted at the pilot. "What the hell are you waiting for?"

"You got it." The pilot, wearing dark wraparound sunglasses and a bright blue baseball cap, released the brakes and gunned the engines hard. The plane surged forward, picking up speed rapidly. They were airborne almost before Blake could get the cockpit door shut.

Blake dropped into the seat behind the pilot, wiping sweat from his forehead with a shaking hand. "Jesus," he said in a hoarse voice, looking down at the village receding rapidly below them. "That was a little too close." He turned back to look for Winters, somewhere behind him. "Are you okay?"

She made no answer. She was staring wide-eyed at the rear of the plane. Blake looked up to see the door to the cargo hatch slowly coming open. The barrel of a chrome-plated .45 automatic appeared first, followed by the head and shoulders of Amos Sanford.

Sanford grinned as he crawled awkwardly out of the small compartment, keeping the gun trained on them. "You all just stay calm now," he said. "We'll have a nice quiet trip back to Port Moresby." He smiled at Blake. "And a nice quiet talk on the way. I bet you've got a lot to tell us, don't you, boy?"

To the pilot, Sanford said, "Straight down to Moresby, Max. Never mind Hagen. I'll keep an eye on Blake here while you drive."

"Sure thing, Mr. Sanford. Be about eighty minutes." The pilot took off his dark glasses. With a shock, Blake recognized him as one of the two men who'd come for him on the very first day.

The pilot winked at Blake. "What happened back there, fella? Forget to pay your hotel bill or something?"

# CHAPTER TWENTY-THREE

Sanford put his head down close to Winters' and spoke over the roar of the engines. "You get the data module, honey?"

She nodded. "Blake's got it. In the pack."

"Show me."

Blake reached over and unzipped the rucksack. The black metal of the module lay exposed. Sanford peered at it. He reached over, popped open the cover, and stared at the data drive inside. "Not very impressive, is it?" he said after a moment.

He looked up at Blake, and then across at Winters, seated beside him. "You two look like pure hell, you know that? What happened? And where's Ed and Ray?" He kept the gun trained on Blake's chest as he spoke.

"They're dead, Amos," said Winters quietly. "Ray Corley double-crossed us."

Rapidly, she recounted what had happened on the mountain. When she was through, Sanford gave a low whistle.

"Well, shit," he said finally. "Tell you the truth, I never figured Ray for a security risk. Still, you got the module, and that's the important thing. How did Blake behave himself?"

Winters looked across at him. "If it weren't for Blake," she said evenly, "we wouldn't be here."

"Anybody left alive up there?"

She shook her head.

"Good. That makes things easier. Nobody in that goddamn village is gonna be able to get word out about this before tomorrow or the next day at the earliest. I had Max here sabotage that Islander at Mount Hagen airport that was due to fly up later today." He chuckled. "We'll be back in Queensland by this evening, just as soon's we pick up Spike in Port Moresby." He shouted forward to the pilot, "How are we fixed for fuel, son?"

"Enough to Townsville, Mr. Sanford," Max yelled back. "We won't have to refuel when we make the pickup in Moresby. We'll hit Somerset on the Cape York Peninsula about three hours after we leave the coast."

Sanford nodded in satisfaction and turned back to Blake. "There's only one loose end here," he said, frowning. "You're supposed to be dead, son."

Blake looked at him. "Did you tell Ed Jeffries to kill me?"

"You bet I did," said Sanford. "Only after you'd found the data module, of course. Couldn't have you running around loose after that, could we?" He glanced at the pilot. "What you reckon, Max?"

Max glanced down at the thick rainforest slipping by beneath the plane. "Do it here, Mr. Sanford," he said. "You won't find a better place. They'd never find a body down there, not in a million years."

"Right." Sanford reached over, pushing open the door of the aircraft. Cold air rushed into the cabin. "You did a good job, Blake," he yelled over the roar of the wind. "No hard feelings. It's just a shitty business we're in, that's all." He raised the gun.

A shot echoed deafeningly inside the tiny cabin, and the plane gave a lurch as the weight shifted suddenly.

Sanford fell heavily to the floor, blood pumping from the wound in his chest. There was a look of utter amazement on his face as his .45 dropped from his lifeless fingers.

Winters turned then, placing the barrel of her gun against the back of Max's neck. "Don't move, or you're dead too," she said. Without turning, she said to Blake, "Throw him out."

Blake stared at her. "What?"

"Throw him out, Peter," she repeated. "Or I'll do it myself. Hurry!"

Blake dragged Sanford's heavy body to the open door and stared down at the ground. Three thousand feet below them, the trees moved slowly by, not a sign of life visible anywhere. Taking a deep breath, he shoved Sanford out. The body fell in the bright crystal sunlight, turning elegant cartwheels in the air. Blake watched until at last the forest canopy swallowed it up. Then he reached over and took the gun from Winters' trembling hand.

Max's face was pale with fear and shock. "For the love of Mike," he croaked at Winters. "You just killed Amos. You shot him and shoved him out the goddamn door! We're on the same team, for Christ's sake!"

"She's not on your team anymore," said Blake, keeping the gun trained on the back of his head. "She never really was. Now shut up and drive the plane. Otherwise, the same thing happens to you."

He turned to Winters. "Shut the door, will you? It's getting cold in here."

* * *

An hour later, the suburbs of Port Moresby came up over the horizon. Max reached for the radio mike, but drew back his hand at a sharp command from Blake.

"I've got to get landing clearance," Max said.

"You won't need it where we're going," Blake replied.

"What do you mean, Peter?" said Winters.

"See the Parliament Building over there?" He pointed ahead of them, at the Waigani government complex, coming up on their right. "There's a nice big highway,

162

hardly ever used, that runs up to it from Waigani Drive. We're going to land on that."

She frowned. "Do you think it's safe to use?"

"Safer than the airport," he replied. "That's where Spike's waiting, remember? Put us down on the highway," he said to Max. "And keep your hand off the microphone."

"Shit, man, you're not supposed to land on roads," Max said. "Suppose we hit a car or something?"

"Stop talking," growled Blake, jamming the gun hard against his neck. "There's nobody on the road right now. Just get us down. Now."

The Islander dropped in low over the deserted highway, wheels almost brushing the tops of the rain trees along Waigani Drive. They hit the road with a hard bounce, Max working the brakes hard to get the plane stopped as fast as possible.

They shuddered to a stop in the middle of the highway, near a grove of trees, far from the Parliament Building and the government complex behind it. The motor died away, leaving nothing but the sounds of insects in the trees and the pinging of the hot metal of the engine.

Blake opened the door and jumped out. Setting the rucksack on the ground, he turned to help Winters down. He saw Max, a throwing knife in his hand, raise his arm behind her back.

"Get down!" Blake shouted, raising the gun.

She started, then dropped to her knees, giving him a clear field of fire. He squeezed off one shot, hitting Max squarely in the forehead. The cockpit windows reddened with sprayed blood as the man pitched over onto his face.

Blake dropped the gun and rushed forward, gathering Winters in his arms. "Are you all right?"

She nodded, trembling against him. "That was a very near thing," she said. "Thank you."

Blake raised his eyes to Max's body, sprawled half out of the cockpit. Disengaging himself from Winters, he said,

"Help me get him out of here. We'll take him over there, under the trees."

She nodded, and together they dragged Max from the plane and across the tarmac, concealing him in some brush at the edge of the trees.

"There's no time to hide him properly," Blake said. "Leave him here and let's move out."

Walking back toward the plane, he picked up the rucksack where he had dropped it, slinging it over his shoulder. "Let's go," he said. "We've got to—"

Blake stopped, open-mouthed, and stared at her. She'd picked up the gun from where he'd dropped it, and now she held it steady in both hands, pointed directly at him. Above the muzzle of the gun, her expression was tense.

"What the hell?" His voice was a croak.

"Change of plan, Peter," she said in a broken voice. "I'm sorry. I really am. Bring the rucksack over here, please."

She raised the gun slightly. There were tears brimming in her eyes. "And when you've done that, get away from here. Run. Please. As fast as you can."

# CHAPTER TWENTY-FOUR

Blake handed over the rucksack, keeping a wary eye on the gun.

"You'd better explain," he said.

Winters' expression was defiant. "The Germans you saw on the mountain weren't the only ones involved, Peter." She glanced around. "They were only part of the team. There are others, and they'll be here soon. They were shadowing Sanford's men, and so they'll know we've landed. You need to leave while you still have the chance." Her face softened. "I didn't want it to end this way, Peter. Believe me."

He stared at her. "You're working for the Germans? I can't believe that."

She tossed her head angrily. "I'm working for myself, Peter. As far as the Germans are concerned, I'm just the messenger. It's simple – I get them what they want, and they pay me."

"Then the money – those euros we found in the rucksack. That–"

"Was for me... Well, me and Ray."

"Wait – Ray Corley was in on this, too?"

"Ray and I worked it out together. We planned it, he and I. Right from the start." She took a deep breath. The gun didn't waver. "After we got fired, Amos Sanford got in touch with Ray, and told him what he wanted to do to Boomer's project. Ray called me, and that's when we got the idea. It was never about Amos Sanford; he just made it possible to get the data module. Sanford had the money to organize things, get us both out to Port Moresby, finance the equipment, all that. But neither Ray nor I trusted him an inch. So, before Ray brought the satellite down, we worked a deal with this German company instead."

She hefted the rucksack. "What's in here is going to set me free, Peter. It's not a fortune, but it's enough to get me a fresh start. And that's all I really want."

"Jesus, Jill–"

"I know, Peter. I know. It didn't work out like I planned, not at all. Oh, the first part went smoothly enough. I called them from Mount Hagen, once I knew what airstrip we'd be flying into."

"You called from the Lodge. That time you went out for a cigarette."

"You almost caught me," she said. "The plan was simple. Ray and I would find the data module, and the German team would meet us on the mountain. We'd do an exchange – money for the data drive. Figuring out what to do with Ed Jeffries was the only real problem."

"So it was you who let the rope go slack that first day. When we were crossing the stream."

"It was both of us, Peter. Ray and me together. We didn't need Jeffries for anything, and we knew he'd be trouble."

"Christ, that's cold. He could have died."

She tossed her head back and looked at him defiantly. "By the time we got into the jungle, the stakes were way too high for good sportsmanship, Peter, don't you think? I'm sure you can see that. Do you really think that Jeffries was going to play fair, in the end? Or that Amos would?"

She looked past Blake, up the road at something behind him. "We sent him into the river, that's true. Later, I was the one who sabotaged the transmitter. And when we'd climbed the rock wall, I turned on the signal beam. I was going to tell you, Peter, just as soon as we'd found the data module. Give you a chance to escape. But then Ray got sick, and the storm came along. Things didn't work out the way we'd planned."

"No," said Blake. "They certainly didn't."

She raised the gun. "And now you've got to leave, Peter. Get out of here. Get far away, before the others come."

Blake looked at her. "You won't shoot me, Jill," he said softly. "Not after all that's happened – all we've been through."

She was crying now. "No, Peter, I won't shoot you," she said. "But someone else probably will." She cocked her head, listening. "Go. They're coming now."

Blake turned to see a car approaching down the empty highway. "Jill, listen to me," he said urgently. "You don't have to give them the data module. You don't have to give them anything. Come with me – now. We can run – there's still time."

Tears spilled slowly down her cheeks. "Run? I'm tired of running, Peter. I've got to do this, don't you see? Then I'll be free. Then it will all be over."

"You'll be dead," Blake snapped. "Do you think your German friends will treat you any differently than Jeffries did? Both of us know too much to stay alive."

"All they want is the data, Peter." Her voice was low and desperate.

"That's exactly right," Blake said. "All they want is the data. Everything else is expendable. That includes both of us."

She looked at him, anguish in her face. "Peter, I have to do this."

He took two steps toward her and put his hands on her shoulders. She lowered her head as he hugged her gently, her chest heaving with small sobs.

"I'll stay, then," he said at last. "Maybe it's time to stop running. If I leave now, you'll die. And I couldn't bear that."

She raised her eyes to his.

"Time to fight now," he whispered. "Together. All or nothing."

She nodded. "All or nothing."

Together, they turned to face the approaching car.

The car stopped in front of them, and the door opened. A heavyset European in a dark business suit got out, looking uncomfortable in the heat.

"Where is it?" His voice was soft and carried only a hint of accent. His eyes were unreadable behind dark glasses, but Blake saw the corner of his mouth twitch as he spoke.

Winters lifted the rucksack. "In here."

The man's tongue darted briefly across his lower lip. "Excellent. Where are the others?"

"There was trouble," said Winters quietly. The German's gaze flickered momentarily across the bloody windows of the Islander's cockpit behind them. "Everyone else is dead," she said after a moment.

"Our team as well?"

Winters nodded.

"*Schade*." He turned his eyes to Blake. "And who is this?"

"He's not with us. He's got nothing to do with this. You can let him go." She still clutched the gun, Blake saw, her knuckles white with strain.

The German seemed to sigh. "The other Americans," he said. "They, too, are dead?"

She nodded.

The man seemed to consider this for a moment. "Well, that makes things much simpler, I suppose," he said thoughtfully. "And do you still have the money?"

"Yes. Yes, thank you, I do."

"You will give it to me, please," said the German. "All of it. And the data module, too, of course."

Blake looked at the gun in Winters' hand, and then up to her stricken eyes. "Shoot him," he whispered. "Shoot him now."

The German had already begun to move when Winters raised the gun and fired. Her shot went wide. She fired again, and they heard a dry click as the hammer snapped against an empty chamber.

The gun was empty.

The German drew a small automatic from his jacket. "Bad luck," he said simply. He levelled the gun at Blake.

"Look, he's got nothing to do with this," Winters said desperately. "Let him go. Please. You'll have the money and the data, damn you – what more do you want?"

The man's eyebrows went up. "I'm sorry," he said. "I'm afraid my instructions were quite explicit. There are to be no survivors. None." He raised his gun.

From the side, a shot rang out. A look of pain and surprise flashed across the German's face, and then he crumpled to the ground. Blood began to seep from under his expensive suit onto the tarmac.

Spike stepped from the trees, a gun in his hand. "Interesting," he said with a tight smile as he walked toward them. "Very interesting. Sanford's gonna love this."

# CHAPTER TWENTY-FIVE

"Sanford's dead," said Blake, watching the gun carefully. "So's Max. Everyone's dead. We're the only ones left."

Spike's eyes swept the scene, lingering momentarily on the blood inside the cockpit. He gave a low whistle. "So that's Max, huh?"

He shook his head. "Nice mess you guys made. Writing up this report's gonna be a bitch." He took a step toward them. "Let's have the sack, then."

Blake stepped back a pace. "What's going to happen then, Spike? Are you going to kill us, like Sanford tried to do?"

Spike smiled broadly. "You won't feel a thing, Blake. Scout's honor." He extended his hand to Winters. "Now give me the fuckin' sack, okay?"

Things happened then with terrifying speed. Winters swung the rucksack, catching Spike full in the face. Roaring with pain, he dropped to his knees. At the same time, Blake launched himself toward the German's gun, lying ten feet away beside the blood-soaked body.

He hit the ground short, rolled over twice and came up in a crouch with the gun in his hand. It was too late. Spike had Winters in an armlock, his gun pointed at her head.

"Freeze, Blake," Spike hissed. He crabbed sideways, keeping her body in front of him. "Drop the gun or I'll shoot her."

Blake shook his head and stood up, keeping his own gun trained on Spike. "No," he said. "You won't. She's the only one who can download the data in that module. Without her, it's garbage. Let her go."

Spike laughed. "In that case, she's coming with me. Move back, man. Now!" Keeping the gun hard against Winters' temple, he walked her over to where the rucksack lay on the ground. He twisted her arm hard, bending her over and making her cry out. "Pick it up, bitch," he croaked.

She gathered up the rucksack, holding it against her like a newborn baby.

Breath hissing, Spike walked her back to the plane. "Get in," he snapped.

From the cockpit, Spike turned to face Blake, standing helplessly below him on the tarmac. "Your girlfriend's my insurance, Blake, my ticket out." He grinned. "I always said I could fly a plane one-handed."

Spike swung the cockpit door shut, and a moment later the Islander's engines coughed into life. Blake blinked against the dust as the plane swung around.

Spike's head appeared in the window. "It isn't over for you, Blake," he yelled above the roar. "Sooner or later, we'll be coming back for you. There's nowhere you can go where we won't find you. Believe it." He grinned again, and the aircraft began to lumber down the road.

Knuckles white on the gun, Blake stood rooted to the spot, watching as the plane moved away. Halfway down the road, the cockpit door flew open. Blake heard two popping sounds over the roar of the props, and a second later, Winters' body fell out onto the tarmac. Good Christ, he thought; Spike's shot her.

Blake raced to the German's car, thirty feet away, wrenched the door open and found the keys in the ignition. He started the car and gunned the motor. The Islander was turning around at the far end of the highway now, revving its motors for takeoff.

Blake slammed the gearshift of the car into first and pressed the accelerator to the floor. One chance left, he thought; one last thing to do. Spike was the last of them. If he got away, the game would go on and on, and he was tired of games. Time to end it.

Tires squealing, he fishtailed down the road, directly in the path of the oncoming plane.

The Islander shimmered in the heat haze as it began to come up along the tarmac, growing closer by the second. Blake shifted into third, gaining speed fast, and heard the motor roar in protest. Now he could see Spike's astonished face in the cockpit window as the two machines raced towards each other. The Islander was picking up speed, nearly at takeoff point now. Above the pounding of his blood, Blake could hear the thundering of the twin props as the aircraft bore down on him.

The side window of the cockpit opened. Twin flashes winked in the sunlight, and Blake's windshield went opaque as bullets slammed into it, crazing the glass. Cursing, he lashed out with his gun, clearing a hole through the broken glass. The roar from the engines was deafening now.

The Islander left the ground. The angle of the airframe changed as the nose came up sharply, impossibly close now, the wheels swinging up and clear as Spike hauled back on the controls. Blake gave a cry of despair.

His last clear image was of Spike's grinning face, just before the tail of the plane scraped the car's roof. A scream of tearing metal filled Blake's ears, and he was slammed hard against the steering wheel. Behind him, several tons of dead weight hit the highway with a thundering crash.

Blake's car lay stalled on the tarmac, its top ripped open. His mouth was full of crushed glass from the windshield, and he realized that he must have been screaming at the moment of impact. He crawled out and limped back to the plane. The Islander lay nose-down on the tarmac, its propellers broken off. One wing was crumpled, and from the wreckage came the raw stink of aviation fuel. Already, a puddle of gasoline was spreading out below the plane from its ruptured tanks.

Wrenching the cockpit door open, he found Spike still strapped in his seat, his face covered with blood and his neck at an odd angle. Beside him was the rucksack. From somewhere underneath the plane came the smell of burning.

Blake snatched up the rucksack and began to run down the highway to where Winters lay motionless. Something's wrong with my leg, he thought irritably – it kept folding up, pitching him to the ground and making him have to get up and start running all over again. His vision was also wrong, somehow – it kept blurring, and objects seemed to recede and advance to the rhythm of his pounding heart. His ears were filled with a keening noise.

After an eternity, he reached her. Dropping to his knees beside her body, he saw that she was still alive and breathing. "Jill," he whispered. "Jill, can you hear me?"

Her eyes fluttered uncertainly and then opened, widening as she recognized him. "Peter. Peter, be careful. He–"

"He's dead," Blake whispered. "Spike's dead. It's over; all over now. Everything's finished."

Pain clouded her eyes, and her lips moved weakly as she tried to speak. "I tried to get the gun," she whispered. "But he shot me. It hurts, Peter. It hurts so much–"

He kissed her forehead gently and staggered to his feet, waving to the police cars approaching down the road toward them.

Turning to reassure her, he was knocked flat as the Islander exploded with a roar, sending a huge fireball high into the air.

# CHAPTER TWENTY-SIX

Blake pointed across the desk at the prime minister's secretary. "Get him out of here," he said. "The cop can stay if you want. But find a tape recorder; you'll want a record of all this later on."

As he waited, Blake surveyed the room. The prime minister's inner office was all understated elegance, paneled with dark wood and furnished with comfortable chairs. On the walls hung a few plaques and photographs, nothing showy. The only odd note was the spear that was mounted on the wall directly behind the prime minister's desk. It was of black palm, Blake noted, with a wickedly carved barbed tip. Almost identical, he thought with a shiver, to the spear Imea had used on the Indonesian soldier, up in the jungle.

A few minutes later a recorder was brought in, and Blake began.

He gave them everything: names, dates, places. Everything he could remember. The data module, its dull metal case dented and scratched, sat between them on the polished teak desk, mute witness to his testimony.

Neither the prime minister nor his chief of security interrupted Blake's monologue. They listened first with disbelief, and then with horror, as the story of the ordeal in the Star Mountains unfolded. Halfway through the narrative, the security officer took Blake's handcuffs off.

When he had finished talking, there was absolute silence in the room. Blake slumped back, exhausted, and closed his eyes, letting the pain and the tiredness wash over him.

The telephone rang. The security officer snatched it up and listened for a moment. He put the phone down and turned to Blake. "The woman is in intensive care. She has a concussion and a punctured lung from the gunshot wound. Her condition is critical but stable, and they are confident that she will survive."

Blake grunted, not opening his eyes.

The prime minister finally rose from behind his desk and came forward, his fingertips brushing the module as he did so. He was a small dark-skinned man, dressed in sandals, a tailored sarong and a print shirt. The shirt was open at the neck to reveal a necklace of dog teeth. His squat bulk was made more impressive by his spade beard and his penetrating eyes, radiating shrewdness and intelligence.

He coughed discreetly, and Blake opened his eyes.

"Mr., ah, Blake," he said, "this is indeed a most shocking and terrible story that you have just told us. I would never have imagined such a thing in my wildest dreams. Still, you obviously speak the truth. The proof" – he glanced at the module – "is here before us. To say nothing of your physical condition. We will arrange for medical attention straight away, of course. But first, a simple question or two."

Blake's numbing fatigue was setting in, and it was becoming difficult to hold his head up.

The prime minister paced back and forth for a moment, hands clasped behind his back. "You really have told a most extraordinary story, Mr. Blake. Let me see if I have understood it all correctly. This, ah, module that you have brought contains information about mineral deposits somewhere here in the country. Is that right?"

Blake nodded.

"Now, about the information contained here," continued the prime minister. "Of what value is it, precisely?"

"That's pretty obvious," said Blake. "It shows you exactly where those mineral deposits are. Believing there's nickel or chromium buried somewhere up in the mountains doesn't do you any good – you could search for years and not find it. Once the information in that module is downloaded and decrypted, you'll know not only what's up there, but you'll know exactly where it is." He looked at the prime minister. "I'd say it's valuable, all right – a lot of people are dead because of it."

The prime minister frowned. "Yes, of course. Very regrettable, I must say. And this, ah, data can be downloaded here?"

"It can. Provided the woman recovers. She's the one who designed the encryption system, and she's the only one who knows how to extract the data and decrypt it."

Blake leaned forward. He spoke quietly and forcefully. "These are strategic minerals, sir, I don't think I need to tell you how important they are going to be to the rest of the world. Most of the emerging green industries depend on these." He tapped the module. "What's in here can give you an enormous economic advantage in the years to come."

"Yes, I can see that." The prime minister walked back behind his desk. His eyes had become bright, Blake noted. After a moment, he coughed quietly and said, "Well, Mr. Blake, this is all extremely interesting. No doubt appropriate measures will have to be taken. You are a very courageous man, and your story is a shocking one." He touched the module. "It was very good of you, of course, to come here and give us this piece of equipment. That goes without saying." He took a deep breath. "There are, however, a great many diplomatic and legal problems here, and I must say in all honesty that in your case, I cannot really see what–"

Blake sighed and pulled himself upright in his chair. "Maybe I haven't made myself clear." He reached over and opened the module, revealing the empty compartment. "I'm not giving you the data, Mr. Prime Minister. I'm selling it."

# CHAPTER TWENTY-SEVEN

The last of the supplies had been loaded on board the Laurabada the night before. Everything had been checked, and checked again. Now they approached the ketch in Blake's small outboard, moving slowly across the absolutely still lagoon in the delicate light of dawn. Overhead, seabirds flew in a ragged line south, toward an unknown destination.

Jill Winters hugged him as they crossed the lagoon. "You never told me, Peter," she said, "about the boat's name."

"Laurabada? It's the local name for the trade wind. The coastal people rely on it to get them out into the world." He grinned. "Kind of like us."

The palms on shore almost hid the outlines of the village, set back from the beach in their shade. All of the big fishing canoes lay on the beach, waiting for the new day. The village was wakening; across the water, Blake could hear the soft laughter of the women as they lit the cooking fires, and occasionally, the barking of a dog or the cry of a child.

Approaching the Laurabada, Blake gazed out to sea, his thoughts wandering in and out among the columns of the past. Drifting back to that day six months ago in the prime minister's office. He had bargained hard, and it had been gratifying, really, how quickly the prime minister had come to understand the situation.

In certain cases, information was most valuable when other people didn't know it. Sanford himself would have agreed with that, Blake knew. And the prime minister had been a good sport afterwards, laughing as heartily as any of the others when Blake told him how he had hidden the small data drive in the grass beside the airstrip, just before the police arrived.

In the end, he and Winters had gotten everything they'd wanted: passports, a safe place to live, and money. Half a million Australian dollars, in an overseas bank account. Blake hadn't thought it necessary to mention the German money, of course.

They'd taken their time picking out a place to hide. Finally it had been Tau, the prime minister's security chief, that suggested his father's village in the Milne Bay Province, southeast of Port Moresby. A day's journey by outrigger from the coastal trading station of Samarai, the village was small, isolated, and secure – there was no way in except on foot or in a canoe.

Over the months, they had become accepted members of the village. In the meantime, Tau and his deputy had quietly cleaned up the mess they'd left behind. A few inquiries had come from the remaining members of Sanford's group, but eventually, they gave up. The dead Germans seemed to have belonged to no one, at least no one wishing to claim them. From the Indonesian side, there had been nothing but silence.

Meanwhile they had furnished their thatched hut with a kerosene fridge, a shortwave radio, books and a portable typewriter. They gardened and fished, and supplies came in once a month from the trading store down the coast. In the evenings, Blake typed.

It's a good life, Blake thought. A quiet life. From time to time, they would get notes from Tau. The last one had said, 'All is well. We have seen no one. Give warm regards to my father and his wives.'

With Winters' help, the prime minister's people had downloaded the data. It pinpointed substantial deposits of half a dozen strategic minerals lying across the Bismarck and Schrader Ranges near the northern coast. The government was now negotiating, hard and carefully, with several international firms for exploitation rights, patents, and joint technical projects. Blake wondered if anyone ever mentioned what all that had cost in lives.

Winters leaned over and kissed him. "Penny for your thoughts, Peter."

He smiled at her. She was once again the striking beauty he had first seen that night so long ago, when they had planned their expedition into the Stars. But there had been changes, of course: she wore the puckered scar of the bullet-wound high on her back, and one of her fingers had lost two joints to frostbite. And there had been a certain indefinable change in her deep green eyes. Call it maturity, he thought, reaching over to stroke her hair.

"Sorry, sweetheart," he said. "Reliving the past, I guess."

She shivered, her eyes clouding slightly. "Don't, Peter. It's over."

He leaned forward to kiss her. "I know. It's just that sometimes, I–"

She put a finger to his lips. "Peter. All the Americans who knew about the operation are dead. So are the Germans." She looked into his eyes. "It'll be almost impossible for anyone else to piece together what happened. Even if they do, the organizations involved won't want to risk publicity. It wouldn't make any sense to come looking for us now."

"What about good old-fashioned revenge?"

Her eyes narrowed. "Don't forget your book; the one you sent to the lawyers in Sydney. If one of us gets killed, they go public with the whole story. Peter, the international business community knows the value of keeping secrets, believe me."

She pulled him close and kissed him hard. "It's a fresh start, Peter. We've got new names and new passports, and a whole new life in front of us." She smiled. "We're rich, we're living in a tropical paradise, and the prettiest girl in the village is in love with you. Or hadn't you noticed?"

They had reached the Laurabada. Blake tied the boat fast to the side, and helped Winters up on deck. "And now we're about to leave our Garden of Eden for the wide world beyond," he said. "Does it bother you that we never got around to deciding exactly what port of call to head for?"

She shook her head. "Not at all. Let's just go. We've got time, Peter. All the time in the world."

Quickly, they raised the sail, catching the fresh morning breeze. Blake stood at the wheel, looking up past the lagoon to where the clouds were massed inland, over the distant ranges. Somewhere up there were the Star Mountains, and the peak the villagers had called 'the place where people die'.

And so many people have died, he thought.

Glancing behind him one last time, he raised his hand in a farewell gesture to memories of the cold wind high on Antares's summit, memories of the night, of the terror. Then he turned away, shivering slightly, and sailed out of the lagoon and into the vast open sea, his heart filling with the infinite promise of the early morning.


The End

If you enjoyed this book, please let others know by leaving a quick review on Amazon. Also, if you spot anything untoward in the paperback, get in touch. We strive for the best quality and appreciate reader feedback.

editor@thebookfolks.com

www.thebookfolks.com

# More fiction by Riall Nolan

## ONE BEATS THE BUSH

Vietnam vet Max Donovan discovers his war-time buddy
has been accused of murder. Suspecting his friend has
been framed and unable to come up with the bail money,
he must solve the case himself. The feathers of a rare bird
were found near the crime scene, and Donovan heads into
the dangerous jungles of Papua New Guinea and the
shark-infested waters of the Coral Sea to discover the
truth.

## WITH TOOTH AND NAIL

When a hitman kills a policeman and makes his getaway by stealing Max Donovan's car, the army veteran makes chase. His quarry is a cunning and violent man heading for another kill and won't welcome Donovan's efforts to stop him. A thrilling game of cat and mouse in the jungle and savannah of Senegal ensues. Only one man will come out on top.

## THE SERPENT'S LAIR

Donovan has survived a bomb explosion in Colombo, Sri Lanka, but is handed a powder keg in the form of a mission to protect the author of a manuscript detailing insurrectionist plans. He's up against powerful forces, not least the ocean and jungle, that he'll have to strike at the heart to subdue.

*FREE with Kindle Unlimited and available in paperback!*

# Other titles of interest

**BOUND TO RUN**
**by Robert McCracken**

A romantic getaway in a remote Lake District cottage turns into a desperate fight for survival for Alex Chase. If she can get away from her pursuer, and that's a big if, she'll be able to concentrate on the burning question in her mind: how to get revenge.

*FREE with Kindle Unlimited and available in paperback!*

## THE HUNTER'S QUARRY
### by Mark West

Young single mother Rachel has no idea why an assassin is trying to kill her. Have they confused her with someone else? Did she do something wrong? Whatever the answer, it looks like they'll carry on trying unless she can get to safety or turn the tables on them. But first she'll have to find out what they want from her.

*FREE with Kindle Unlimited and available in paperback!*

*Sign up to our mailing list to find out about new releases and special offers!*

**www.thebookfolks.com**

Made in United States
North Haven, CT
15 June 2024

53626120R00117